*Kay
Thanks for you
in all you do. God Bless!*

E. nuf sed

HE WHO LIVES
BY THE SWORD

A STREET PARABLE

A NOVEL BY
E. NUF SED

PublishAmerica
Baltimore

First printing

All characters appearing in this work are fictitious. Any resemblance to real persons, living or dead, is purely coincidental.

ISBN: 1-4241-6359-5
PUBLISHED BY PUBLISHAMERICA, LLLP
www.publishamerica.com
Baltimore

Printed in the United States of America

DEDICATION

This book is solely dedicated to the memory of my beloved mother, Vivian Zina Anderson (1953 1990). Mom, next to God, you've been the most important inspiration of my life. I hope I've made you proud thus far. You may have never believed me when I told you, but you were always my favorite girl. You will always and forever stay in my heart. I love you.

To my family members who have passed on to a better place:

Elmore Rembert Sr.; Earnestine Mable Rembert; Kevan Fletcher; Kevin Simpson; Vernon "Tat" Hazel; Brandon Christopher Davis (My baby brother); Reverend Dr. Harold Nash; and my good friend Eric Garrison.

Rest in Peace.

ACKNOWLEDGMENTS

First and foremost, I would like to give thanks to my Lord and Savior, Jesus Christ, for blessing me with the talent and opportunity to share my gift to the world. It's been a long, hard, continuous struggle, but I know you indeed have a purpose for my life. I will forever continue to keep your praises in my mouth and your joy in my heart.

Secondly, I give thanks to my late mother, Vivian Zina Anderson, to whom this book is dedicated. Words cannot describe the influence you have had in my life. You made me into the man I am today and for that I'm forever grateful. No one could ever take your place Mom, Ever! I love you always, Mommy.

To my late Big-Momma, Earnestine Mable Rembert, I'm equally thankful. Thank you for your no-nonsense upbringing and constant caring and love that brought me to where I am today. You were the most righteous woman I've ever known, seriously. I love you always, Grandma.

Thanks to my Pops, Kenneth Neal Anderson Sr., for your constant support and funny stories over the years. You've been there for me when it counted and I'll never forget that. I know you don't like my pen name, but that's who I am now; no disrespect to the name you gave me. Though you don't always say it, it's nice to know I've made you proud. I love you, Pops.

To my one and only sister, Kacey Anderson, what can I say, I owe you the world, girl. Thank you for the long talks and laughter that kept me going when times were rough. You've been more than just a sister to me, you've been my best friend. Love Ya!

Much love to my daughters, Jenay and Kierra. Without y'all, none of this would matter. You're the reason I do what I do, remember that! Daddy loves his little angels forever. Yes, Jenay, no matter how old you think you are, you're still my angel.

To my nieces, Kayla and Lyneea; my nephew, Brandon; my extended family, Aaron, Tamia, Alexia, Dasia, Megan, and my new Goddaughter, Madison, I love all of you like I love my own children. Never hesitate to ask Uncle Kay for anything. Be good and remember that education is always the key.

To Aunt Gail, thanks for being a big sister to me over the years. I could always count on you to be there for me. Anything you need, I got your back, baby. Love ya!

To Uncle June, get ya mind right, man! Seriously, I hope you get yourself together, man, because I care about you. Thanks for your funny (hilarious) stories over the years. You should've been a comedian, man. I'm praying for you, Unc.

To my ex-wifey, Tammy, I know we're not the best of friends, but I thank you for giving me a beautiful daughter and for showing me that, "pain is love." Good luck in all you do.

To Tanya, thank you also for giving me a beautiful daughter and your constant support. Though we're not really friends anymore, you were my first love, as well as the mother of my first child and for that alone I'm extremely grateful. Hopefully we'll be able to see eye to eye one day.

Tiea, I saved the best T for last, baby (Ha-Ha). Thanks for all your support and motivation during the writing of this novel. We did it, baby! Couldn't have done it without you. Thank you for giving me a beautiful baby boy (I hope). This is just the beginning, baby. Love you, Boo!

To all my co-workers at D.O.C., thanks for y'all support, criticism, and jokes. Not bad for a "Dummy", huh? I know y'all meant well. Good luck in all your endeavors.

I like to give an extra special thanks to the city that raised me, Baltimore, Maryland. Edmondson Village "Stand Up!" More importantly for not letting me become a victim of its streets. To me, B-More is still a beautiful city to live. We just have to start raising our kids with the right values. We will rise again B-More, B-Lieve That!

To Ralph E. Johnson, that's for giving a brotha an opportunity to shine and for introducing me to the literary world. I won't disappoint you "Big Bra." C.O.'s unite.

To Jay, even though you crossed me, bra, thanks for introducing me to the spoken word; without that background, I would have never known I had the ability to write. Maybe one day I'll have the strength to forgive you. Don't hold ya breath, though.

To anyone I may have forgotten, just know that you're not out of my heart, just my mind right now, so don't take it personal. This one's definitely for the streets y'all...LET'S GO!

Psalms 23:4-6

Yea though I walk through the valley of the shadow of death, I will fear no evil: for thou art with me; thou rod and thy staff they comfort me. Thou prepares a table before me in the presence of mine enemies: thou anointest my head with oil; my cup runneth over. Surely goodness and mercy shall follow me all the days of my life: and I will dwell in the house of the Lord forever.

Amen

INTRODUCTION

In any major crime syndicate, there is an enforcer, a person one must answer to if things don't go as planned. In urban crime cartels, such enforcers are called "hitmen." Situations such as monies coming up short, products missing or speculation of talks with the police will get you a deadly date with the hitman. For the most part, hitmen aren't very nice people. They are usually socially withdrawn, emotionally repressed, apathetic creatures that take money for what they probably like doing for free...Murdering! In the grimy streets of Baltimore, justice doesn't prevail in the courts, it often prevails in the streets, with death being the most favorable sentence. Hustlers high on the food chain don't want to risk life in prison or life on the run while in the process of handling necessary business, so often times hired help is needed. That's where the hitman comes in. Street assassins may range in age from 15 to 75, there's no age restrictions in murder for hire. Only the desire to get the target quick and fast and without notice. There's no training required either for this position, only heart, and not a caring one either, one that doesn't pump "Kool Aid." To succeed in the murder for hire game, one has to be totally and equal ably prepared to deal with all consequences of the underground life, even death. You live by one rule and one rule only, don't miss!

It is a common myth that hitmen are big, ugly, goons with low IQs. Nothing could be further from the truth. Assassins today are smarter than Rocket Scientist, employing any tactic to destroy their target. Sometimes hitmen aren't even men at all. Sometimes they come in sweet, pretty little packages. They could be sexy and seductive, at the same time dangerous and deadly. Female assassins could be just as heartless and effective as any ugly goon from the lowest parts of the Earth. Even worse, because you never see them coming. So, if you ever find yourself in the unfortunate position of having a price on your head, Beware! Your next-door babysitter could be the one that comes to collect.

CHAPTER ONE: PAYBACK TIME

"It's payback time, you rat bastard!" were the words uttered from the Grim Reaper's mouth as he chewed on a split wooden toothpick that was dangling from the sides of his lips. Inconspicuously positioned inside an abandoned row house on Baltimore's West Lafayette Street, Reap waited for Dukes to leave his son's mother's apartment building so he could put in his day's work and collect his pay. Reap's choice of weapon for this particular job was a sweet chrome Desert Eagle .357 Magnum, equipped with silencer of course. His "down bitch" as he affectionately called it, always managed to get the job done right quick and efficiently the first time.

As Reap patiently waited for his target to unexpectedly meet his fate, he wondered how Dukes, one of Alonzo's most devoted workers, could betray them all. It had been long speculated that Dukes might be an informant for a made undercover cop looking to shutdown Alonzo's lucrative $30,000-a-day operation. On more than one occasion, Dukes had been seen talking to and even taking rides with the unfamiliar out-of-towner who was supposed to be his, "man from up north", Newark, New Jersey, to be exact. Dukes vouched for the Jake real heavy and no one ever questioned Duke's integrity until this one grimy kid, "Luck", said that Duke's man from up north busted him three years ago for three pills of dope.

"I'd know that motherfucka anywhere," Luck said with so much conviction in his weed-glazed eyes. "Cocksucka made me strip butt-ass naked on the avenue in the middle of fuckin' December, in zero fuckin' degree weather for three fuckin' pills of dope. Had me just laying there on that cold ass pavement for an hour. Bitch took my money and talked major shit to me right in my face. Yeah, I'd recognize that motherfucka anywhere, and Dukes ain't shit for fuckin' with him."

Luck was as grimy as they came, so neither Alonzo nor any of his operatives whole-heartedly believed him, but they watched Dukes like a near-sighted hawk. Nothing happened for a while, but when a surprise bust came in on one of Alonzo's major drug houses, everyone knew that Dukes was a backstabbing, bitch-ass rat that had to die. Nevertheless, being the shrewd businessman Alonzo was, he knew that there might be an inkling of truth to what Luck said, therefore he shut down shop and emptied out product in every manufacturing and stash house located in the Westside precinct. When the police raided the houses, nothing incriminating was found. The bust was a complete failure and once again Five-O had nothing on Alonzo or his staff.

An hour later, Dukes exited the apartment building walking with a quick stride. The block was vacant, minus a zoned-out dope fiend struggling to stand against the apartment building's tag-infested walls. Totally oblivious to the fact that he was the hunted, Dukes gave a last proud fatherly wave to Davon, who was playfully peeking out of the third floor window blinds at his father. Dukes lip synced, "I love you" affectionately to his son and proceeded to touch the door handle of his pearl white Q-45. Simultaneously, a loud blast broke the silence of the block, "Boom!" Dukes stopped in his tracks as his brains spattered on the car's smoke-gray tinted windows as he hit the asphalt with a lifeless thud. The dope fiend on cloud nine continued his effortless lean without so much as a flinch and Davon seemed to disappear out the blinds where he just seconds ago waved his final good-bye to his ill-fated father. The abandoned row home Reap previously occupied was now vacant without a trace that anyone had ever trespassed in it. The Grim Reaper had successfully struck again without anyone seeing a glimpse of him. He was an all too familiar reality in the cold streets of Baltimore.

CHAPTER TWO: THE PAYOFF

As Alonzo reclined in his soft, Corinthian leather Lazy- Boy, he tensely massaged his temples and began to strategize on how he was going to rebound from his all-to-close infiltration. This was the first time any of his workers had ever been disloyal to him and it troubled him badly that Dukes would have to pay with his life for his betrayal. Alonzo was a laid back, easy-going cat who considered himself more of an entrepreneur than a hustler. He lived in a $400,000 split-level house in a secluded, gated community in Owings Mills because he wanted to live among the well-to-do upper class; doctors, lawyers, corporate-heads, shit like that. He was an educated brother with a bachelor's degree in business management from Bowie State and may have been well on his way to a promising career, maybe as a CEO of a successful Fortune 500 company, if he wasn't so damn good at marketing drugs. Drugs started out as an experiment to

HE WHO LIVES BY THE SWORD
A STREET PARABLE

Alonzo, a quick way he and his college roommate, Eric, could pay off some nagging tuition debts and have some extra pocket change. They invested in a pound of weed and exclusively sold dime bags to known weed-heads on campus. Alonzo and Eric were the best and damn near only access to a high within a five-mile radius of Bowie, so needless to say, they became synonymous with partying on campus. On any given night, Zo and Eric would effortlessly go through a pound of their product, leaving less time for academics and more time to supply for the increasing demand of their bombing weed. Both of them would go days at a time without going to any of their classes, which sparked curiosity among the staff, especially Zo's professors because he was regarded as one of the brighter students in most of his classes. Zo's academic status began to drastically slip to the point of him being a prime candidate for academic probation.

Far to proud to flunk out of college, Zo decided to put his education on the back-burner and go into the drug business full-throttle. Eric was less dedicated to the game and concentrated a little more on his studies, being awakened by the fact that he could be thrown out of school soon and waste the tuition money his mother had struggled all his life to afford. Eric took his half of the profits and bailed out of the drug business in pursuit of an education. Alonzo took his share of their profits and set up shop in a surrounding area of Bowie. He employed some financially struggling ex-school mates to run for him at the campus and in town.

Zo marketed his product relentlessly and before long, he had all of Bowie as well as the outskirt counties of D.C. on lock. Establishing rep in Southern Maryland allowed Zo to set up major connections in D.C. and Baltimore, which quickly upped his clientele and product. He began to invest in Coke and

Heroine and was just as successful in marketing them as marijuana. Alonzo was now a certified Baller and was on his way to making major moves in the drug game. Through connections, Zo heard of an area in Baltimore that was hot and prime for the taking, minus a few minor hustlers he could easily put on his payroll. He relocated in West Baltimore and within weeks had it jumping. Alonzo's shit was the best shit around pound for pound in West Baltimore and he quickly established himself as a major player in the entire city.

Alonzo was awakened from his thoughts by the melodic chime of his doorbell. Peeking out through his silk drapes, he was pleased to see who was standing on the other side of the door.

"Good ol' Reap. Like the Marc Train, comes through every time."

Alonzo swiftly opened the solid redwood door to greet Reap.

"You're here earlier than I expected." Alonzo glanced at Reap with a slight look of disdain. "I hope that means business is taken care of."

"Isn't it always?" Reap replied with an emotionless tone and a look of seriousness in his eyes.

"Always coming through like the motherfuckin' Marc Train." Alonzo's disposition instantly transformed into jovial mode. "That's why I only fuck with you in fucked up situations like this. It's like you have the ability to separate your personal feelings and get work done. I know you were cool with Dukes, shit, I was too. Hurt me to my heart it had to come to this, but I couldn't let him ruin the operation Reap. All that we worked so hard to build."

Reap stood unaffected by Zo's words. Zo then proceeded to walk downstairs into a spacious room he called his office. In it was a desk, chair and computer along with shelves containing what seemed like every book ever written, from literary masterpieces to thick books on Human Psychology and Behaviors. Zo was an avid reader and had knowledge of various subjects. Zo removed a thick book about the slave trade from the shelf, which exposed a small titanium safe. Methodically, he positioned the numbers on the dial, opening the safe and exposing several bricks of cash stacked as to resemble a barrier around the inside of the safe. He removed a brick of one hundred dollar bills and handed them to his dependable contractor.

"Does this shit ever get to you, Reap?" Alonzo asked with concern.

"Nope, just business as usual." Reap responded with the same dryness he originally greeted Zo with. "The day I start taking this shit personal is the day I'll quit."

Reap put his brick of ten G's inside the small leather backpack he always carried when it was time to collect his money. He and Alonzo engaged in a few more trivial words before Reap headed to the door. Walking to his black, chromed out late model Pathfinder, Reap couldn't help but to think about how he was now ten thousand dollars closer to his big plans of business ownership and retirement from the game.

As Reap entered his comfortably furnished, two-bedroom bachelor pad, he followed his same nightly routine. He fed his three enormous Jack Dempsey tropical fish which he loved so much because of their aggressiveness. He checked his phone messages, which were usually none except for business calls, since he didn't have many friends. Next, he grabbed an ice-cold chocolate Yoo-hoo out the frig and reclined in his black leather Jennifer Convertible chair. He turned on his 60-inch big screen just in time to catch the 11:00 p.m. news reporting a fatal shooting in West Baltimore-Duke's murder. His son's mother was performing for the news cameras, crying and sobbing, talking about how someone could do something like this to her son's father, he had no enemies. They even had the nerve to have his three-year old son on camera crying and shit. The whole scene made Reap sick to his stomach. He always thought it was disgusting how the media exploited the victims family on TV all emotional. The only reason for it was to show how impoverished and ignorant black people sometimes were in the midst of tragedy. The news further reported that there were no leads as of yet in the murder, which didn't surprise Reap because he always kept his shit "air tight." There were no fingerprints, no shells, no reliable witnesses.

Reap took his brick of money out of the backpack and put it in a metal lock-box in his closet containing $20,000 more. He never kept all of his money in one place, nor large amounts in the bank accounts in order to keep away suspicion. Yes, contract killing had definitely been good to Reap over the past years, and he was damn good at it too. However, he had far bigger goals to achieve. Dreams of enterprising and ownership constantly filled his head. He thought about opening his own Bounty Hunting business or Private Investigating service. After all, Reap had the reputation of always getting his man. As he grabbed his gun cleaning kit and began to clean the Desert Eagle from the day's events, Reap contentedly smiled and thought about how he came to be what he was, a Stone Cold Killer.

CHAPTER THREE: IN THE BEGINNING

It was graduation day, June 1990, and Marco Raymond proceeded across the auditorium stage to receive his diploma. Though it didn't show on the outside, this was the proudest moment in young Marco's life. He had graduated with honors from one of the most prestigious high schools in Baltimore City, The Baltimore Polytechnical Institute, and now it was time for him to be all he could be in the United States Navy. None could be prouder of Marco than his mother Regina. It had been just her and Marco since his father left them when Marco was four. Her son was all she had and she put every bit of effort that she had into raising and instilling manhood into him.

Only eighteen years apart, Regina and Marco were more like sister and brother than mother and son. It would be nothing for them to hang at the movies all day or go bike riding in the park exclusively and have fun as if they were childhood friends. Regina knew that she would deeply miss her son when he left for the Navy, but she also knew that she had to cut the apron strings and let Marco come into manhood on his own. It would be the hardest thing she had to do in her life.

Also in attendance at the graduation were Marco's on again, off again father, Roland, grandmother Tuesday May, Aunt Grace, and Chay, the second most love of Marco's life. Marco and Chay shared a special kind of puppy love that they swore nobody would break, not even four years of separation. Marco even proposed to her on Valentine's Day with a $100 Value City 14 karat gold ring. Nobody, especially Regina, liked the idea of Marco even thinking about marriage at such a young age, but he was determined to make Chay his bride once he settled in the service.

Marco and Regina's relationship greatly diminished, mainly because Regina wasn't used to Marco spending all his time with someone else. For years, her son was the only man in her life, so him taking such deep interest in a young lady took some getting used to. After all, Regina thought nobody was good enough for Marco. After various arguments, Regina accepted the fact that her little boy was now a man in love and that Chay was very much a part of his life. Before long, Regina and Chay became like mother and daughter. Regina even started dating again to subside the loneliness.

In August, Marco departed for Great Lakes, Illinois for Navy boot camp. Desert storm had just kicked off, so Marco knew that upon graduation he would probably be shipped off to the Persian Golf to fight some white man's war for God knows what. His intentions were to travel and get a free education from the Navy; at least that was what he was made to belief by the bullshit commercials and the lying ass recruiter. However, through no fault of his own, World War III conveniently broke out after his hasty enlistment and there was no way Marco could retract his patriotic obligations. Although he tried hard not to show it on the outside, Marco was nervous and scared, especially leaving behind the two women he cared most about in the world.

In the airport seconds before boarding, Regina hugged her son as if she would never see him again in life. She gave Marco a wallet-sized picture of her with writing on the back that said, "No matter where you are in the world, I'll always be with you. Love you always." Then tears hurriedly fell down Regina's face. It hurt her to be temporarily losing her only son.

It was nightfall when Marco stepped off the bus onto the Boot Camp base. Tired from the hour-long plane ride, the additional hour wait at O'Hare Airport for the shuttle and the ride to the base, Marco was in no mood for bullshit. He wanted a hot meal and a good night's sleep. As soon as they stepped off the shuttle, the group of fresh face recruits were greeted by a short, stocky, arrogant white Petty Officer First Class with an anger management problem.

"Alright, you mothafuckas, grab your shit and walk to the barracks on your right. Find a bunk, shit, shower and shave and hit the rack; you'll have a long day tomorrow."

The group hustled off fast, as if a bomb exploded on the base. Marco laid in his bed that night staring up at the ceiling until the wee hours of the morning thinking, "What have I gotten myself into?"

As a month passed, Marco got used to the military life and had even taken a liken to it. He had been designated to be the leader of his company, always got the highest possible score on his physical training test and was even recommended for S.E.A.L. training by his chief company commander. Though staying focused took Marco's mind from being homesick, he still made it a point to call Regina and Chay every night to tell his favorite women how much he was missing them. On boot camp graduation day, Regina, Regina's boyfriend Glenn, and Chay drove 13 hours from Baltimore to Chicago to spend the weekend with Marco. He had graduated at the top of his company and was receiving special recognition for his accomplishments. Furthermore, Marco had passed his Seal physical screening test on the first try with an outstanding score, which meant he was well on his way to becoming one of the elite Navy Seals. Marco felt like he was on top of the world, and finally seeing Regina and Chay added fuel to his inner fire. As he spotted them among the crowd of visitors, he quickly embraced them both with so much passion they nearly passed out from suffocation. Marco loved the fact that he had a whole weekend of unrestricted liberty and planned to spend every second of it with the women he loved.

Two o' clock in the morning Marco and Chay were awakened from their blissful sleep by a frantic knock on their hotel room door.

"Wake up Marc, I really need your help." The voice was that of Regina's and she was panicking. "Come on Marc, wake up."

Marco hurriedly opened the door confused and concerned. His mother stared at him in tears and desperation. "Glenn is drunk and locked himself in the bathroom. We got into an argument tonight by the pool and now he's threatening to kill himself."

Marco ran to the adjacent room and frantically knocked on the bathroom door. He heard a loud, uncontrollable gag and bang on the walls as if someone was fighting for their life. Suddenly, a loud crash hit the bathroom door and wood splinters went flying everywhere. Glenn fell from the torn down sprinkler head in the bathroom with a tight fitting noose tied around his neck. He was crying and gagging uncontrollably.

"What the fuck is going on?" Marco looked at the whole scene in total disbelief. He always knew Glenn was a little strange, but this shit was wilder than anything he could ever imagine Glenn would do.

"She don't love me, I know she don't love me." Glenn had a blank, psychotic look on his face. His knuckles were bleeding badly from where he was banging on the walls from his near-death experience. Regina sat by his side comforting him with mixed feelings of fear and concern on her face. Of all the men in Baltimore she could've dated, she chose a crazy mothafucka. Chicago police ran through the door like a murder just occurred. They took one look at the scene and concluded that Marco must've beat the shit outta Glenn. Without any questions, they forced Marco into the wall and slapped handcuffs on his wrist.

"Get the fuck off my son!" Regina snapped out of her sentimental mode and was now in kick-ass mode. "He didn't do anything, Glenn did this to himself!" Regina shouted, pointing at the dazed-out man on the floor.

The police stared at Regina with a confused, Barney Fife look. "Are you sure that's what happened, ma'am?"

"Yes, I'm sure. Now let my son go."

Chicago's finest took the cuffs off Marco and placed them on Glenn's wrist. They said they were taking him to the station for questioning and in the meantime Regina, Marco and Chay would have to find another hotel, since that one wanted them out for destroying their property. This was indeed a horrible night for Marco.

The next couple of days, Marco and Chay had to spend heavy quality time with each other in the Best Western hotel on the other side of Chicago, the only hotel they were able to find with vacancies. Since that was graduation week, every horny sailor in Great Lakes hurried to hotels throughout town to sow their wild oats. Regina spent the whole weekend visiting Glenn at the local hospital. After he sobered up, he left the police station and checked himself into the hospital to repair his wounds and his mind. This wasn't the first time he felt like ending it all.

Lately with all his financial problems and his insecurities about Regina, Glenn had been an emotional wreck. He felt as if he was developing a severe nervous breakdown. Whenever he drank, his depressions and desperations seemed to increase. Regina did her best to try to help him cope with his demons but she was near her wits end. The only thing keeping her with him was the fear that if she left, he would hurt himself. Regina couldn't handle that on her conscious, so therefore she decided to help Glenn get psychiatric help for his depression and whenever he progressed, she would bounce. Having a deranged, emotionally unstable boyfriend wasn't her idea of love.

When it was time for them to leave Great Lakes, Marco begged Regina to let him catch the plane home and leave Glenn's crazy ass in Chicago, admitted to a mental institution. Regina couldn't be that cruel. She insisted on driving back to Chicago from Baltimore to pick them both up. It just wasn't in her heart to leave Glenn helpless like that. Before his depression, she had grown used to his companionship and thought it was only right to fully be there for her man.

During the thirteen or so hours back to Baltimore, the three nearly sat in silence in the car. Marco now looked at Glenn as a total nutcase and his mother as stupid for supporting a nutcase. He thought about his mother's safety with such a man and if he ever did anything to hurt her how he would happily go to prison for the rest of his life for the satisfaction of murdering him. Briefly, these were his thoughts. Then his mind focused on the sweet satisfaction of coming home for two weeks after two months of intense boot camp brainwashing. He thought about how much he missed Chay and the sweet tender love they would make upon his arrival. He thought about finally eating a good home cooked meal after two months of slop, and taking a long, hot shower instead of a short, ice-cold one. He thought about being a civilian again for two weeks and smiled.

For the next two weeks Marco and Chay spent time together talking, laughing, going out and making love. Marco had only spent one day with his mother but couldn't stand the fact that Glenn called day and night for her and she still talked to him. Wasn't it enough that he ruined his graduation? He wanted Glenn to stay the fuck out of his mother's life and ruin someone else's. Regina felt Marco's concern, but explained to him that it wasn't that easy to cut Glenn completely off. While Marco was in boot camp, she had taken a routine visit to her GYN and found out she was three weeks pregnant. Always wanting to have another child and not believing in abortion left little options for Regina. She wanted desperately for Glenn to be in her unborn child's life but not hers. The news of this devastated Marco. He didn't know whether to be joyous or disappointed in Regina for allowing herself to get into such a situation. Growing up the only child, Marco had always wanted a baby brother or sister, but not at the expense of his mother's happiness. It would have to take him awhile to get used to this new revelation, but somewhere down the line he knew crazy-ass Glenn would have to go. He would be the child's father figure if need be.

After Marco's short vacation home, Regina thought it

would be a good idea to drive Marco to his next military assignment; his advanced school(A school). Damn Neck, Virginia was a small military town near Virginia Beach, three hours from Baltimore. This would give Regina and Marco the quality time they missed with each other when he was home. They talked, laughed and made plans for the baby together. They thought of names for him and even talked about Regina and the baby coming to live with him when he was stationed permanently. Marco would soon have an additional person to love just as much as he loved his two favorite women, and it felt pretty good.

When they arrived in Damn Neck, Marco gave his mother an airtight hug for what seemed like an eternity. He rubbed his "hope to be" little brother and slowly exited the car with held back tears in his eyes. It was now time to get back to discipline and regiment for him. To make it worse, none of his boot camp buddies were at his school, so he would have to go through the process of making new friends, which he hated. You would always have to go through the process of weeding out who was real and who was fake.

Marco's first two weeks of A school was a breeze. It was all basic math and graph plotting. He aced his first test and passed every inspection with an outstanding rating. By week three, Marco felt homesick. He called Regina and told her he was coming home for the weekend.

"You just got there, save your money," she affectionately told him. "Next weekend Chay and I'll drive up and get you."

Marco was cool with that and told his mother how much success he was having in A school. She was pleased. She told him all the happenings at home. She had caught Glenn in bed with another woman and decided to leave his cheating, crazy ass alone for good. She was relieved that she finally had an excuse to leave the relationship for good without feeling guilty. She would be alone again, but at least happy. None was happier than Marco to hear the news. Finally, he knew his mother was out of harm's way and he could stop worrying about her so much.

Early Sunday morning Marco called home for some money. The night before, he had gambled what little he had away on card games and needed a little boost until payday. He thought it strange that by 8:00a.m. Regina wasn't home. She worked the night shift 11:00 p.m. to 7:00 a.m. at the local jail as a correctional officer, a job she moved from Baltimore to Jessup, Maryland to work. Marco figured she must've gone to his grandmother's house after work as she sometimes did, therefore, he continued on with his day. It was his duty day anyway and he wasn't allowed to leave his barracks.

That night on watch, Marco decided to call Chay. He knew he wasn't supposed to be on the phone during his watch but what the hell, he had the mid-watch, so everyone was sleep. Marco got excited the minute he heard Chay's voice, but something in her voice didn't sound right. She began screaming and acting hysterical. Everyone in the house seemed to be. Chay's mother took the phone from her and told Marco to get his Officer in Charge. Marco knew from the tone in her voice that this wasn't good. Marco ran downstairs past the officer on watch to get the Officer in Charge. He was so nervous and frantic when the officer answered the door that all he could say was AI got some bad news on the phone and they wanna talk to you. Seeing his disposition, the Officer complied. The Officer in Charge took the news from Chay's mother and silently handed Marco the phone. He then wearily told Marco to sit down. Marco was scared. The news given to him by Ms. Greene hit him like an arrow in his heart. Regina had been tragically killed. Shot to death by Glenn in a murder-suicide. Glenn had come to her job early that morning after a night full of drunken rage and depression, and shot her twice, once in the head, once in the chest. Then fatally turned the gun on himself, blowing his brains out. It wasn't hard for him to get a weapon in the jail. After all, he was a veteran Lieutenant in corrections and wasn't questioned by the outside tower officer when he showed up to work on his day off. In fact, the officer issued him a standard .38 caliber pistol and watched him enter through the entrance of the institution, forgetting that no weapons or ammunition were permitted beyond that point. Nothing was said. Ten minutes later, three deafening shots filled the basement of the maximum security prison. "Boom! Boom! Boom!" In an instant, Glenn had ended his worthless, pathetic life as well as Regina's and her unborn baby's. Glenn had finally gone off the deep end and did the ultimate. He forever sealed his and Regina's destiny with a single desperate act of cowardliness.

Marco felt paralyzed at the first reaction of the horrific news. He couldn't believe Regina and his unborn baby brother had been killed at the hands of a deranged lunatic that he wanted his mother to stay away from in the first place. Marco felt like he was to blame. He always knew that if he left Regina alone with that maniac he would do something crazy to her. Marco felt guilty. Then instantly felt rage. Violently he turned over a row of wall lockers in the berthing area, disturbing the night's peace. Not relieved, he grabbed a metal chair and threw it against the fragile wall of the barracks, waking everyone in the berthing. When a concerned student tried to calm him down, Marco leveled him with a smashing right hook to the jaw and stomped him repeatedly on the floor. He was officially out of control. It took a couple of MP's to finally restrain Marco and stop him from his self destruction.

Marco was excused from the incident primarily because of his tragic losses. The next day he was flown home to grieve and prepare for his mother's funeral. It took everything he had in him for him to compose himself as he watched Regina's body get lowered into the Earth. For the first time ever, Marco felt helpless and all alone. He thought about abandoning the Navy and staying home to help his family stay strong. The death had been especially hard on his grandmother. Regina was her oldest and most dependable child. However, deep inside, Marco knew he had to finish what he had started; Regina would have wanted it that way.

Marco returned to Damn Neck and three months later graduated A school. The next day he was flown to Coronado, California to start SEAL training. Though still very much a soldier at heart, Marco was now a loner. He rarely smiled, didn't talk much and had no friends. He focused all his time and energy on his military task at hand. The first eight weeks of training, he conditioned his body with calisthenics, running obstacle courses, and long, intense ocean swims. The second phase of his training qualified him as a combat diver. He was conditioned to swim two miles in the ocean with full scuba gear on, and could break a neck underwater if need be.

Marco was trained in all phases of ground warfare and excelled in them all. From explosives to fighting strategies, from rappelling off a cliff, to land navigation, he was a natural. His true talent though was in his shooting. Every target practice, every qualification, every mission simulation, Marco would picture Glenn's face staring back at him. He would then draw back a blank, becoming oblivious to his surroundings. His eyes would squint, his breathing would stop, his pulse would race, making whatever he aimed at a perfect dead on shot. Many of his fellow soldiers, mostly white, were amazed by Marco's accomplishments. Some were jealous and thought him to be a head case. Nevertheless, all respected him and his ability to accomplish the Navy's mission. All except one.

Besides speaking when spoken to, Marco developed a habit of silence. It was an almost eerie disposition of solitude. No one, not even his Unit Commander, knew anything about him. He was a total mystery. One night, approximately one week from graduation, Marco passed a group of his white comrades while walking to the shower. "Nigger thinks he's better than us," he heard one boldly say as if he didn't care if Marco heard. "He don't even belong here." Marco became so accustomed to hearing these remarks for the last seven months from the white boys on his unit that he became unaffected by their words. However, sometimes he had to mentally restrain himself. Marco flipped over his dog tags and looked at his mother's picture for inspiration and endurance. He had to do this for time to time to stay motivated.

As Marco proceeded on his path, he heard the voice again. "That bitch's picture he wears on the back of his dog tags must give the nigger power, as much as he looks at it," the voice said amusingly, referring to the picture of Regina Marco wore on the back of his dog tags. Without warning, the head belonging to the voice was cracked with a metal chair. Unable to retaliate, the blasphemous bloodied skull was repeatedly hit against the metal lockers he was standing against just moments ago. The other white boys tried to pull Marco from their fallen friend but to no avail. His ass belonged to Marco. Alerts were called, alarms were sounded. It didn't matter. This time, it took damn near half a squadron to pull Marco from his victim and the other half to calm him down.

Marco had beaten his fellow soldier within an inch of his life. The man would spend the next three months in intensive care, drinking his lunch through a straw; Marco would spend his next six months in the Brig. Upon release, Marco would get a bad conduct discharge from the Navy, later upgraded to a medical discharge for evaluated psychological reasons. He would return to the streets of Baltimore with nothing but the shirt on his back. Angry and bitter, Marco tried to rekindle his relationship with Chay. It wouldn't work, He was no longer the man she knew. He was replaced by an angry, insensitive, socially withdrawn loser that she wanted nothing to do with. She didn't even bother to tell him about the miscarriage she had when he was away, fearing it would be too hard for him to take.

There was one thing Marco managed to keep; his love for guns. With the insurance money he collected from Regina's death, Marco invested in every firearm you could think of, from 9mm's to .45s, from sawed-off shotguns to .308 Winchester riffles. He even had a M-16 rifle like the one he was issued in the Navy. He read every publication he could find on weaponry. It got to the point where he could break any weapon down and put it back together again in the dark. He became compulsive. His house was an arsenal.

One day in the local gun shop, while talking weaponry with the store clerk, Marco met an up and coming street hustler named Alonzo, who was intrigued by his thorough knowledge of guns. The two talked extensively and found that they each had an interest in each other's professions.

CHAPTER FOUR: POLITICS AS USUAL

Councilman Steven McCullough stared at the pile of back dated mail stacked on his already overcrowded desk. It had been a long day for him and he was desperately ready to end it and go home. At this time, nothing sounded better to him than an ice-cold beer, a hot dinner and a warm night's sleep. However, there was still work to be done.

McCullough opened one of the letters dated a week ago. He quickly read it and then tossed it in a corner of his overly cluttered desk. It was yet another complaint by a resident of the 4th district of Baltimore about the excessive drug selling and thug loitering in her neighborhood. These letters had become a routine to McCullough, and to be frank, he was growing quite sick of them. He knew drugs had been and always would be a part of Baltimore's neighborhoods and there was little or nothing he or any other politician could do to stop that. Besides, he was on Alonzo's payroll to do exactly what he had been doing, nothing.

For years, he, along with other crooked politicians and dirty cops, kept bare minimal police patrol and surveillances of Alonzo's territories. Request of him for higher police presence in neighborhoods had been virtually ignored. Meetings with him by residents were far and few in between, and even less productive. McCullough's district had pretty much become and open-air drug market. He was indeed a typical politician and an integral part of Alonzo's operation. However, with the upcoming elections and ever growing complaints from his constituents, McCullough knew that he would have to make some drastic changes in his district regarding his stand on drugs, but not before first talking to Alonzo.

Councilman McCullough called Alonzo's two-way. He told him that it was important that they meet somewhere tonight to discuss some crucial business matters. Given the fact that McCullough rarely called him for anything, Alonzo had to assume that something was wrong and agreed to meet him at an old abandoned warehouse in Fells Point. It would take him an hour.

When McCullough arrived at the warehouse, the jet-black and chrome 600 S-Class was already there, lights dimmed, waiting in the shadows. McCullough pulled his Town car parallel to the Benz and got out. Alonzo did the same.

"Councilman, what's the deal my man? Ain't seen you in awhile," Alonzo said, greeting the councilman and extending his hand for a shake. Councilman McCullough extended his hand to Alonzo's. "Yeah I know. Just making laws and hitting bars," McCullough said in his usual uptight and corny way. He was a stuffy, white undercover Redneck not socially comfortable around blacks outside of work, unless, of course, it was benefitting him. "Look, we gotta talk. You know over the past four years I've been looking out for ya and letting ya do ya thang with no problem. I'd scratch ya back, you'd scratch mines and everything always ran al'ight. You always respected my position and I'm grateful for that, but we got a problem." McCullough sighed before continuing. "Election time's coming and I'm really in the hot seat. People getting tired of the drugs and trafficking on their streets; they want me to do something about it soon Alonzo, and for my career sake, I have to appear that I am."

Alonzo appeared undisturbed by the councilman's words. He knew this time would come when his "Aces" would have to really do their jobs and he prepared for it. He would simply cut back product around that district and focus on another long enough to content the neighborhoods. When he informed McCullough of his strategy, the councilman seemed unmoved by his solution.

"It's not that simple Alonzo. Ya see there's starting to be a lot of speculation that I'm dealing with ya. A couple folks have even come to me about a pay off to keep them quiet about me and ya. Of course, I've denied the allegations, but people ain't stupid. They know and they got their hands in my pocket Alonzo. Like I said Alonzo, ya always scratched my back and I've scratched yours, but now mines is getting itchier. I've put my job on the line for years for ya, and now it's time to up the ante."

Alonzo surprised, yet still unaffected, leaned back on his freshly waxed 6. "Like I said councilman, I'll pull out your district for a minute, but I'm not laying down no more cheese, I don't need you that much." McCullough stared at Alonzo with a sinister look. With a Slave Master like smirk on his face, he responded, "It would be a huge move for me in reelection if your operation was somehow shut-down and your ass indicted. I would be the hero of the 4th district in Baltimore City, and you'll be just another fucking convicted drug dealer." Alonzo's whole disposition changed. He didn't like threats, or even worse bribes, especially coming from a useless, fat greedy, racist pig like McCullough. Alonzo would have to play this out. Obviously outwitted, Alonzo scratched his head. " No need for threats. This could be mutually worked out. Saturday I'm throwing a big party on my yacht. We're leaving from Annapolis 7:00p.m. Come along, and bring your lovely wife. We'll celebrate our new negotiation." McCullough laughed victoriously. "I knew you would see it my way. You're a smart man, Alonzo, real smart. See you Saturday." The two vehicles drove off in different directions.

Alonzo's yacht was gorgeous. Seventy-five feet in length, it was like a mansion on water. It had everything from an elegant dining hall to a full court basketball gym on it. Everybody from the who's who of celebrities to the big Ballas of the entire East Coast have the privilege to sail on this beauty, and tonight would be no different. The "Heaven Afloat" was packed with the finest and most distinguished company Baltimore had to offer.

Councilman McCullough was enjoying the festivities the "Heaven Afloat" had to offer. Known as a "party animal", he was downing his seventh Martini when Alonzo approached him. "Enjoying yourself, Councilman?" Alonzo said, patting Councilman McCullough on his back. "Hell yeah!" Slightly slurring his speech McCullough threw his arm around Alonzo's shoulder. "Your parties are always the shit, that's why I never miss one."

"Thanks. That's always good to hear." Alonzo smiled and attempted to move on. McCullough jerked Alonzo's shoulder.

"When are we going to discuss business, I don't know how long I can stay sober," McCullough said, laughing as though he just told the funniest joke he ever heard.

"Well, I was gonna tell you later on, but I guess now is a better time than any." Alonzo searched the room for prying eyes. Everyone was having a good time, oblivious to McCullough and Alonzo's conversation. "Meet me on the fantail in about an hour; I'll have what you need then." Alonzo patted McCullough on his shoulder and stepped off in to the crowd of patrons partying on his boat.

McCullough's greediness quickly sobered him up. As instructed, he ventured to the fantail an hour later. As he stated, Alonzo was patiently waiting for him by the rail, in all black. There was not another soul on the back of the yacht except them two. McCullough stumbled towards Alonzo in anticipation. "Let's make this quick Alonzo, I'm drunker than a worm in tequila."

As McCullough arrived face to face with Alonzo, he wondered if his eyes were playing tricks on him. This person that stood before him wasn't Alonzo; he appeared to be bigger and meaner. Before he could say anything, McCullough was hit with a paralyzing blow to the carotid artery in his neck. As he attempted to fall, the stranger caught his body, and with a mighty twist, broke his neck. The stranger then threw McCullough's lifeless body over his shoulder and sprang over the rail into the cold waters of the Chesapeake Bay. No one knew what happened to Councilman McCullough. His death was eventually chalked up to him falling overboard in a drunken accident. His body was never found due to the strong current of the bay and that was one less problem Alonzo had to worry about.

CHAPTER FIVE: THE TAKEOVER

It was a cool, brisk autumn night on Mount St. and as usual the block was hot. Reds, blues, and yellows were as plentiful as skittles and if your fancy was Coke or Weed, the block had you covered too. Young hustlers grinded the strip day in, day out, waiting for their turn at becoming the next Scare face or Nino Brown and would gladly murder a motherfucker who stood in the way of that. To them, this drug game was a way of life, a state of mind and the only key for them obtaining the American Dream. To them, getting money was their law, the streets were their judiciary, G-code was their constitution, and death was their punishment. It was no other way. Dreams of one day becoming "Hood Rich" kept every hustler and hood rat motivated.

On the corner of Mount and Lafayette, a blue, late model Caprice filled with purple haze sat in the midst of the nightly happenings. The four New York cats occupying the smoke-filled car were carefully observing the night's business. They watched the sales, who was selling what and how fast they were selling it. They saw the clientele, the junkies that seemed to come far and wide repetitiously to cop the second grade dope being offered to them. They looked for heat, and noticed the infrequent rounds police made down a block that was oblivious pumping with illegal activities. All these factors added up to vast opportunities in the out-of-towner's minds. They knew that if they offered a product in higher quantity and far better quality than what was being sold on this block, they would be rich in no time. This would be the perfect spot for them they thought. With plenty of night action and limited street soldiers to stop their progress, they would have Baltimore sowed up in no time. All four smiled as they envisioned success and power. Careful as to not be mistaken for snitches or stick-up boys, the Caprice drove off down the block.

A week later, eight deep in a black Suburban, the New York boys made their way down south to Maryland. Equipped with an arsenal of guns, drugs and money, they were determined to make a lasting impression on the new city they planned to take over by storm. These were some real grimy niggas. Though hustlers by choice, they were killas by nature and were used to laying stake to their fame by any means necessary. On more than one occasion, blood baths occurred in the streets at the hands of these guys over nothing more than having the right to make money any fucking where they pleased. If need be, this trip would be no different.

The Suburban hit the block with no lights penetrating the dark street except from the fire of the muzzle of the AR-15's letting off multiple, thunderous shots on the strip. Bystanders scattered like roaches in the midst of screams and shattered glass as the truck sped off down the street. Unable to get a full grip of what happened, the block shut down for the night.

The next night shots rang out again on the block, except now coming from an old Chevy Astro Van. Some frustrated hustlers ran for cover, while others scrambled for their individual guns to bust back at the van but to no avail. The van disappeared in the night quicker than the Suburban did the night before.

For days the block stayed abandoned and in destruction. The hustlers that usually served the strip laid low, trying to find a reason or some justification for the bullshit that kicked off the previous nights. Knowing that no local rivals would be stupid enough to even tread on one of Alonzo's most "money making" strips, they concluded that it had to be out-of-towners looking to takeover. Kwame, the head corner man of the block and Alonzo's younger cousin, wasn't taking this shit lying down. Young and crazy, Kwame was the thug version of Alonzo. He had a reputation of dealing with motherfuckers that fucked with him and his. What he lacked in brains, he more than made up for in heart, and wasn't afraid to die to protect his turf. Kwame was a true up and coming street soldier that was making it on his own strength, not Alonzo's. He had big dreams of making it to the top in this game. He had come too far in the game to let some clown New York cats run him from his destiny. He may have to declare war.

Kwame looked around for abnormalities as he hit the block. Besides the absence of him and his crew hustling the strip, the block looked as if it had returned to normal. The same fiends that paced the block day and night, in search of their next blast, still inhabited the streets. Though it had been some days since

Kwame had served any of them, none of them looked withdrawn or in desperate need of drugs in their systems. This didn't make sense. Kwame needed to know what the fuck was going on.

A figure suddenly appeared on the street. "Renee," Kwame called out to an abused-looking, dark skinned, slender woman swiftly walking out of the corner candy store. "Renee, come here!" Slowing her pace, the woman descended towards Kwame.

"Who serving you?" Kwame asked Renee abruptly with a look on his face that told her that he wasn't to be bullshitted with. Displaying a look of both confusion and fear, Renee answered, "What?"

"You heard me, who serving you?" Kwame repeated with more seriousness in his voice. "Don't bullshit me either."

"What makes you think I copped any drugs, Kwame?"

"C'mon, bitch, I've been knowing you for years, and I know you need that shit in you everyday, can't function without it. And since me and my crew ain't been out here for some days now, you ain't been blasted from us, but you've been blasted. So, for the last time bitch, who fuckin' serving you?"

"I don't want no trouble Kwame."

"Ain't gonna be no trouble, baby girl, as long as you cooperate," Kwame said, forcing a smile. "I'm just trying to see who my competition is." Kwame pulled a twenty bag of dope out of his pants pocket. "I'll make it worth your while shorty."

Almost immediately, Renee snatched the bag of dope, pulled out her needle and filled it with the free heroin she just received from Kwame. Staring at the ground the whole time, she hesitantly mumbled, "Star."

"Who?" Kwame looked at Renee as if she were speaking a foreign language.

"Star! Look, I've never seen him before. He and his crew just started coming round here a couple days ago. Said he had some new shit he wanted us to try since we hadn't seen y'all in a few days and we needed a blast. He called it Galaxy. Good name for it too 'cause the shit was out of this world. "Oh Wee!" Renee momentarily laughed while collapsing in a slight nod, exposing her rotting teeth. "No disrespect, but y'all gonna have to go to the lab if y'all wanna compete with Galaxy 'cause it's shittin' on anything y'all gotta offer. I'm telling you, it's the..."

"Okay!" Kwame stopped Renee mid-sentence. "Where them niggas serving from?"

Renee frightenly looked back at the ground and anxiously scratched her face from the high she was now experiencing. "Look, you ain't heard it from me, okay. They at Karen's apartment. Star gave her $1,000 cash plus paying her rent to set up shop there until he get established down here. He must be a New York boy or some'in cause he don't seem to know Baltimore too good. He keep asking where this and that is. Got a New York accent, too. About six of 'em in Karen's apartment, but I swear, Kwame, don't tell nobody I told you, please. You gotta promise me." Renee went back into her nod.

"It's all good, baby girl," Kwame said with a look of satisfaction on his face. "This just between me and you, that's my word, and my word is as good as my dope, or should I say Star's dope. Anyways, good looking out." Kwame walked across the street, leaving Renee engrossed in her drug use and unsure of the fate her mouth might've cost her.

Business was slow in the hood tonight. So slow that Star, Jeep, Pooh, A'min and Lex shut down business out of Karen's roach-infested apartment and retired to the hotel rooms they had on reserve for the two weeks they've been in Baltimore. Business had been good for them during the preceding weeks, but they were tired of chillin' in Junkieville. They wanted a night of good food, good sleep and good sex to break the monotony of the constant grinding they'd been doing day in, day out. They left Buddha at the apartment to handle the infrequent sales of the night and to keep watch of the drugs. After all, they were serving out of a junkie's house, and junkies were never, ever to be trusted.

Buddha was the baby and fuck-boy of Star's crew. He was a short, stocky, nineteen year old kid, hungry to make the grind and a name for himself. He begged Star persistently to be put on for years, but was overlooked because Star wasn't pressed about having little kids on his team. However, Buddha was the type of young'in that was down to do whatever, whenever Star needed him and that in time proved essential for Star. He would keep on using his young protégé until he was used up.

Buddha laid back in a zone, enjoying the blazing headpiece being given to him by Karen. Though a junkie, Karen always managed to stay on top of her trick game as a hustle and she took pride at being one of the best at it. As he watched her thick, juicy lips hungrily gobble up his manhood, Buddha seemed impervious to the sound of the apartment door being kicked in. He even looked almost apathetic as he saw the three masked intruders make their way towards him from the hallway with 9mm Glocks drawn. He was pathetically helpless as he tried to run for cover with his pants still fallen around his ankles. Barely unable to let off a scream, Karen fell face down as the but of a saw-off shotgun smacked across the back of her skull. From there, it's muzzle found it's way under Buddha's scrotum while a Glock 9mm was being forced in his mouth.

"You know what time it is, nigga," the third intruder said. "Where the shit at?"

Without hesitation, Buddha mumbled where the dope and coke could be found in addition to the grand stashed in his front pants pocket. He was scared shitless. Though Buddha had always been down for whatever for Star, he had never been put in a life or death situation before. His youthful vulnerability was beginning to show. Tears began to flow from Buddha's swollen eyes and uncontrollably he began to urinate on the shotgun, which was uncomfortably jammed in his nut-sack.

"You pissing on me, motherfucker!" the intruder holding the sawed-off screamed.

Buddha uncontrollably shook his head and before he could mumble a word, "Blam!" Buddha passed out as blood and flesh spattered from what used to be his groin.

"Are you fuckin' crazy, nigga! That's not how the shit was supposed to go down," the intruder yelled out, simultaneously taking off his mask and still holding the 9mm in Buddha's mouth.

"Shut up, motherfucka! Put that nigga outta his misery and let's get the fuck outta here."

With that command, the intruder squeezed the trigger of the 9mm and blew Buddha's memory on the wall. Next, the three ransacked the apartment, confiscating a few pounds of valve-up coke and bagged-up dope. They took a loaded AR-15 rifle they found in the hallway closet, verifying that they must've been the niggas that cranked on them the two previous nights before. The three men headed towards the apartment door, but one of them detoured back towards the bedroom.

"Boom!" A final deafening shot rang out through the muzzle of the 9mm.

"Damn, nigga, what the fuck did you do now?" one of the men hysterically screamed.

"Leave no witnesses, nigga."

CHAPTER SIX: GIMME THE LOOT

A tear rolled down Renee's eyes as she stared down at her life-long friend. Though they had been strung out on drugs for years, Renee remembered a time when she and Karen were the flyest females in the hood. Dipped in the latest fashions, their hair always looked like they stepped fresh outta the salon. Ballers were the only niggas lucky enough to even be seen with these Ghetto Divas, much less take them out, and if you didn't come correct on the first date with them, you wouldn't have to worry about opening your mouth to speak to them the next time you saw them. Karen and Renee were notoriously "Ghetto Fabulous" and knew the hood was theirs for the taking. They never thought that the hood would eventually take them.

Karen was laid up in University Hospital, head and face totally bandaged from a bullet grazing the back of her skull and exiting through her right cheek. Groggy but conscious, she stared up at Renee's swollen eyes and seemed to be in sync with her friend's thoughts. Renee was overwhelmed by Karen's consciousness. Not knowing the extent of Karen's injuries, she thought it would be weeks before Karen could even move a muscle. Relieved, she wanted desperately to give her friend a big hug and talk with her, but didn't want to risk further trauma to her brain. Still, Renee had to know who was responsible for her friend's pain. She wondered if Karen's memory was still intact. Renee looked down at Karen and softly whispered, "Kwame?" Karen slowly nodded her head.

Back at the hotel, Star violently paced around the two floor suite they reserved at the Wyndham Hotel in downtown Baltimore. Twin 9mm Glocks in hand, he stormed from one room to another, trying to figure his next move. It wasn't the fact that nearly $30,000 of his shit was robbed blind from him that made him on edge. No, being heavy in the drug game, you always had to be prepared to take a loss, whether from police or jealous ass niggas. It wasn't even the fact that his little man had been murdered execution style that made his trigger finger so itchy. In the game, death was all too common and familiar. You learned never to get too attached to someone else in the game, they could be here today, gone tomorrow. What did make Star so angry, so enraged, was the fact that he got played. In little ass, slow ass, country ass Baltimore, a New York nigga got played. He was supposed to take over this fuckin' city. Now he couldn't even show his face on the block because police had it under surveillance. He would no doubt be the number one suspect in a murder/attempted murder trial if anyone in the hood ever caught a glimpse of him again. Star couldn't risk it. In the morning he and his crew would be on 95 North back to New York.

At midnight, Star rounded up his crew and was about to check out of the hotel for good when he received a call on his cell.

"Who dis?" Star answered, not recognizing the number calling him.

"Hello,…um, Star, it's very important that I talk to you, I…"

"Who the fuck is dis?" Star interrupted the caller, growing impatient and pressed for time.

"Dis is Renee. Look Star, I need to talk to you right away, please it's im…"

"Renee who? I don't know any fuckin' Renee!"

"Karen's friend, Star! Look, can we meet, I have to tell you something real important."

"Karen's friend! You junkie bitch, fuck you doing callin' me? You tryin' to set me up?" Star proceeded to end the call, but was stopped short.

"No, but I know who is."

"Talk to me, bitch," Star said with sudden curiosity.

"Not over the phone. Meet me somewhere. I'm over East side at a friends house on Orleans and Rose. Meet me at the 7-Eleven up the street from there in an hour."

"You bet' not be settin' me up, bitch. I'm not for no games, I'll kill…"

"It's not a set-up, Star, please."

"A'ight bet, an hour."

Star hung up his cell feeling stupid about even talking to Renee, much less meeting her. Nevertheless, if she knew something that could better his situation, it might benefit him to hear her out. Star held off the check-out and told his crew to chill. He would be back.

Star pulled up on the 7-Eleven parking lot skeptically looking for heat. When he saw none, he relaxed a bit. Standing over by the pay phones to the left of him he saw a skinny woman wearing a baseball cap pulled down over her eyes and moving fidgety. He concluded that was Renee. He beeped the horn. Renee proceeded to the truck slow and cautiously. Though she knew it was Star, his windows were tinted jet black and she was unsure of his intentions. The driver's side window slowly rolled down.

"Hurry up, I ain't got all day!" Star roared, looking at his platinum timepiece on his wrist. "Get in."

Picking up the pace a bit, Renee jumped in the passenger side of the Suburban.

"Talk," Star said, not even glancing in Renee's direction.

"It was Kwame. He was the man on the block before y'all took over. Said he just wanted to know who his competition was. I didn't know he would..." Renee started crying uncontrollably. "Star, I'm sorry."

Looking unsympathetic, Star asked, "Where dis cat be?"

Renee answered without hesitation, "His girl lives around the corner from Karen's apartment. He be there most of the time when he's hustling. He got a black Lexus that's parked in the front when he's there."

"Show me." Star, still unmoved by Renee's testimony, proceeded off the parking lot and headed back to the hood. Fifteen minutes later, Star pulled up to a set of row houses on Lafayette.

"There, 2906," Renee said excitedly. "He's not there now, but he comes through every night."

"How you know?" Star asked unconvincingly.

"I'm a dope fiend. I'm up and down the block all night long. I know this neighborhood like the back of my hand. Believe me when I tell you this nigga comes here every night."

"Is it just him and his girl?" Star asked.

"Naw, she has a daughter about ten. Sometimes she stays with her father I think. His girl is always home though. Hardly ever leaves the house."

"Good look," Star said, reaching in his leather jacket for a bag of his notorious Galaxy dope. "Don't tell nobody you saw me."

"Don't tell nobody what I told you. My life's the one in danger. Renee said, retrieving the dope and exiting the Suburban.

"Done," Star replied, driving off into the night.

Four nights later, Kwame pulled up to Quetta's house on Lafayette. He would have some serious explaining to do after being gone for a week. Nevertheless, it was a much needed vacation. Kwame had to get away to clear his head from all the drama that occurred the week before. He seen the murder of the New York boy and the unidentified girl broadcasted all over the news and he instantly got paranoid. Jogging up the front steps, he assumed Quetta had gone to bed since all the lights were out in the house. He figured this was unusually early for her and Sierra to be sleep since ordinarily one of them would be up watching T.V., but since he hadn't been home for a week, they might have changed their habits. He would have to use his key.

Kwame fumbled through his assortment of keys on his key ring to find the key to the house. Being a major playa in the game, Kwame had various keys to other women's cribs on his key ring and sometimes found it difficult to differentiate between them. However, this was the key he used most often. Entering the house, Kwame felt along the hallway wall for the light switch.

"What the fuck!" he screamed as a hand grabbed his before he could turn on the light.

"Shut up, nigga!" Kwame heard a voice yell as a double-barrel shotgun was slammed into his mouth. "Don't mumble a fuckin' word. We gonna do this shit nice and quiet, and everything might be a'ight, understood." Kwame nodded his head.

"Walk back out the motherfuckin' door and slow, nigga!" the voice continued.

Kwame complied as the double-barrel was now shoved in his back. He was led to an old, blue Chevy Astro van by four masked strangers and thrown in the back.

"You know what this is, motherfucka. I hope your man value your fuckin' life." With that said, the van sped off down the street.

The next morning, Quetta would be found by her daughter Sierra returning home from her father's house, her throat cut from ear to ear, with the saying written in blood, "An eye for an eye" scribed above her head. Blocks away, Renee would be found by police, dead from an apparent dosage of bad drugs she just injected the night before. Kwame would be headed up north to New York, held for ransom. Word of mouth indeed travels, and it didn't take long for Star to find out that Kwame's cousin was the hottest shit in B-more. Though his girl had to be sacrificed, for the time being Kwame would live. If word on the streets were true, this nigga was worth a fortune, and that's what it would take if his people ever wanted to see him alive again.

CHAPTER SEVEN: THE SURPRISE

Alonzo shook his head in irritation as once again the Channel 13 News reported on the unsolved murder of an unknown man and the attempted murder of an undisclosed woman inside a West Baltimore apartment last week.

"Stupid fuckin' nigga!" Alonzo lashed out in high volume as if he was scolding the half-naked, chocolate Nubian Goddess that was giving him a full body rub-down as he watched the evening news. "How could he be so stupid?"

It was no secret to Alonzo that his "cowboy" cousin was involved in the murder/attempted murder that was being broadcasted all over the news all week. In fact, when he read the article in the paper the day after it happened, he thought it was something right up Kwame's alley. He knew Kwame was a loose cannon for years, and never would hesitate to lay someone down for hardly any reason at all. In a sense, Alonzo liked that in Kwame because it represented something more powerful that respect—it represented fear. But never in a million years did he think Kwame would put the whole operation in jeopardy with his cockiness.

Word was already on the street that Kwame and his crazy ass squad of killas were the ones that kicked in Karen's door on some revenge shit and murdered everything moving, or so at least they thought. That was another thing. Karen. What if she talked? There was probably a cop posted outside her room around the clock just waiting to pick her for information as soon as she was able to talk. She would definitely finger Kwame, even with masks on, his character was hard to disguise. She only scored crack from him every fuckin' day of her life. Karen would have to be dealt with before she left her hospital bed; that was for certain. But how?

"Relax, you're so tense." Alonzo was distracted from his worries by the sensual voice of the talented masseuse so craftily working out all the kinks in his lower extremities. She was so fine, she would make a doomed man on death row forget about his execution the next day. One look at her, Alonzo briefly forgot about what the hell he was just beefing about. He just closed his eyes and enjoyed his pampering.

Though nights like this came a dime a dozen for Alonzo, Myra was definitely one of a kind, or should he say one of two kinds. Her twin sister Mandie was just as sexy and irresistible as she was. Tonight was her night off. Alonzo had hired them both to massage him as a form of therapeutic relaxation on stressful days like today. On extra stressful days, Zo would enjoy a double serving of Myra and Mandie's soothing rub-downs, usually followed by an all night three-way sexcapade that left him barely able to get outta bed the next morning. Treatments like that could get addictive, and Zo wasn't the type to let pussy overrule business, so Myra and Mandie was a once in a while enjoyment for him. Nevertheless, he was ecstatic to know he was living every straight man's dream.

Alonzo rang Kwame's cell for the third time in the past hour. No answer. This was unlike Kwame. From the moment Zo put him on, Alonzo instilled in Kwame the necessity of communication. Kwame always notified him if he was leaving town, if there was trouble, and definitely if Alonzo called him more than once. This was hustling 101. Since Kwame wasn't answering any of Alonzo's calls, Alonzo decided that he would have to go by his house a little later to make sure Kwame wasn't already knocked off. But first, Alonzo had more pressing issues to deal with. He called Reap on the land line.

"Reap my man, how much you know about chemistry Brother?"

"Chemistry?" Reap was a little thrown back by Alonzo's line of questioning. "I know a little. What you need to know about?"

"Lethal injections." The phone suddenly went silent.

Karen awakened from her sleep in terror. The heart monitor bleeped so swiftly nurses rushed to her room to see if she was having a heart attacked. She wasn't. She had a nightmare. It wasn't the first she had since she was shot, but it was definitely the most realistic. The entire night replayed in Karen's mind, sending vivid images and clear voices to her sub-consciousness. Just like déjà vu Karen saw Kwame's face as he veered down on her helpless body and squeezed the trigger of the long black gun. "Bam!" It felt so real; Karen could even still smell the gunpowder from the gun.

The first restful sleep Karen was able to get in weeks and she was disturbed by an awful nightmare. Most of her nights were spent tossing and turning, trying to cope with her excruciating pain and discomfort she felt whenever her medication wore off. Now the rest of her night was spent with the fear of drifting off to sleep, returning to the nightmare that was now her reality. This was hell for Karen. As devoted as she'd been to Kwame, how could he be the Devil?

Alonzo pulled up in front of Kwame's house in devastation. He thought he must have arrived at the wrong address. With all the yellow caution tape around the front steps and the big pad lock on the door, Alonzo knew his cousin couldn't have been murdered. As big as Kwame was on the streets, word would've gotten to Alonzo within the first ten minutes. But then, where the fuck was Kwame? Alonzo scoured the neighborhood in confusion. He quickly spotted Raheem, a young, petty corner man of the block. Alonzo knew he could get some answers from the kid.

"Yo, Raheem!" Alonzo motioned for the young hustler to approach.

"Yo who dat?" Raheem was hesitant to approach the black Benz with black mirror tint. That was an easy way for a hustling nigga to get dealt with or robbed in the hood. Raheem had made some enemies during his short tour on the block and some of them even threatened to kill him if they ever saw him again. Raheem wasn't taking no chances. "Naw, I'm good."

"Raheem get your little ass over here, it's me, Alonzo! I ain't got no beef with you."

"Oh Zo man, I ain't had nothing to do with that bullshit with your peoples, I swear, man."

"What bullshit Ra. What are you talking about? What happened?" Alonzo responded, now panicking.

"Damn, you haven't heard?" Raheem said, sensing Alonzo's concern and trying to be sensitive. "Man, Kwame's girl got killed last night. Niggas split her throat from ear to ear. Nobody seen Kwame yet, but word is that them same niggas got 'em, Dawg. His car was in front of the house this morning but the police towed it for investigation. In case they find any clues in it and shit."

Alonzo just stared at Raheem with a look of death on his face. He couldn't believe what he was hearing. Quetta was dead! Kwame kidnapped! If this was true, there was no measure to the bloodshed that would take place in retaliation of this. Alonzo thought long and hard. "What about Quetta's daughter?"

"Yo, she was here with the police this morning crying and screaming and shit. It was fucked up to see her like that 'cause she so young. Her father came and calmed her down though. I think she left with him."

Alonzo was distraught by the whole situation, but was relieved that nothing happened to Sierra. It had been enough the cowards had killed a woman, but a child, that shit was forbidden. Alonzo still strongly believed in the age-old code of "Honor among thieves." To kill an innocent child would have been an abomination. Alonzo whispered to himself, "Thank God!" Alonzo slid Raheem a C-note and a pound for the information and sped off up the block. He had enough excitement for one day.

The new nurse swaggered past the nurse station en route to room 536. The floor was so busy, no one seemed to notice how new or how sexy the nurse was that made her way through the congested hallway of the intensive care unit, not even the police officer that was busy being relieved of his shift by another officer. The beautiful nurse smiled as she entered the room, prepared to give her patient her daily medication. With confidence, she injected the solution into the IV of her sleeping patient, careful not to make too much noise as she didn't want to disturb her from her peaceful day's sleep. When the nurse finished medicating her patient, she exited the room as graceful as she entered, still smiling from a job well done.

An hour later, doctors rushed to room 536 in response to a flat line alarm. When they arrived, it was too late. Karen was dead from an apparent heart attack. The autopsy later revealed a high dosage of hydrochloric acid in her blood. Both doctors and nurses were bluffers. Karen was the most watched patient on ICU, how could this have happened?

Alonzo tried hard to relax as Mandie and Myra both massaged Alonzo's back to relieve him from the day's terrible events. Myra still had on the sexy nurse outfit she wore to carry out Alonzo's orders earlier today. Myra and Mandie were far from killers, but when it came to money and Alonzo, they would damn near do anything. Alonzo felt a sense of guilt about what he had done to Karen, in spite of Kwame's possible kidnapping. It was too late to stop Myra, being that she had left for the hospital before Alonzo found out the tragic news of Quetta and Kwame. This was just another sin Alonzo would have to repent for. With a lot on his mind, Alonzo drifted off to sleep trying to forget the drama that was his life.

The melodic chime of Alonzo's doorbell woke him out of his sleep. Is was 12:00 noon and Alonzo wasn't expecting any company. Besides the twins, those that knew him knew better than to pay him a visit unannounced; Alonzo wasn't big on surprises. Nevertheless, still comatose, Alonzo looked through the peephole at who was disturbing his afternoon rest. Whoever was there had left. Thinking that it might have been the postman, Alonzo opened the door. He was right. A small, brown un-addressed box with an un-addressed envelope attached to it laid at the foot of his door.

Alonzo wasn't expecting any mail, so he was skeptical about retrieving the package. One thing he learned about the drug business was that you acquire a lot of so-called friends, as well as enemies, that would like nothing better than to see you dead. Hence, he didn't put the idea of a bomb out of his mind; all was fair in love and drugs. However, going against his better judgment, Alonzo took the envelope attached to the box and opened it. A letter was inside. Alonzo slowly read:

> Dear Rich Nigga,
>
> If you ever want to see your bitch-ass cousin, Kwame, alive again bring you ass to New York with $200,000 by tomorrow night, 10:00 p.m. That's your deadline, nigga, and not a minute past. We'll call you 9:30 and tell you where to bring the dough. No cops and no bullshit or his bitch-ass is dead. To show you we're not bullshitting, we sent you a little token of our sincerity. Enjoy.
>
> Fuck You,
> Real Killas

Alonzo felt paralyzed. His worse nightmare had come to reality. This time the motherfuckas went too far. This time was family, and to Alonzo, family was priceless, especially Kwame. He and Alonzo were like brothers after Kwame's biological brother was killed in a cross-fire two years ago. After that, Kwame and Alonzo swore nothing else tragic would happen to family again, not if they could help it. Yeah, Alonzo would bring the money by tomorrow night like instructed, but he would also bring the pain. That would be very necessary.

Alonzo took a deep breath and prepared for the worst as he opened the small, brown box. The box was filled with Styrofoam balls. Alonzo cautiously shifted through the balls, curious as to the contents. Alonzo felt an object and slowly lifted it out of the box.

"Ah shit!" Alonzo screamed as he fell back and nearly fainted. "What the fuck!"

Alonzo stared in shock at the severed index finger dangling from his own fingers. Still attached was Kwame's diamond platinum ring Alonzo copped him for his last birthday. Alonzo dropped the finger. This was too much for him to handle. Apparently, these niggas meant business and weren't bluffers, He couldn't take the risk of losing his closest blood. Alonzo went to his safe, took out ten bricks of cash and placed them in a briefcase. He then went to his arsenal and packed his twin Glock 32s in the small of his back. Most importantly, he made a final phone call before his unexpected departure. This would be the most important trip of his life.

CHAPTER EIGHT: THE GET-BACK

As Alonzo sped down I-95 North, all he could think about was the safety of his cousin. Tough he knew the way of life he led involved sheisty individuals and deadly situations, it never hit closer to home than now how dangerous this lifestyle was. He had gotten into the game strictly to make money. He put his cousin onto the game strictly to make money. Had he known that the shit would one day escalate to this, he would have stayed in school and made money legitimately.

Alonzo always knew that Kwame would die in the drug game. He took the shit too seriously. Hustling was like a way of life to Kwame; it was a part of his personality. For him, it was beyond all the money, it was life as he saw it. Kwame would gladly die for that shit, and Alonzo hated himself for letting the game take his cousin over.

HE WHO LIVES BY THE SWORD
A STREET PARABLE

Alonzo arrived in Staten Island by four o'clock. He knew a few shot callers there, so he decided to pay some of them a visit to see what they knew about the grimy niggas that kidnapped his family. Somebody was sure to have heard something. Alonzo knew one Baller in particular that would definitely know what was going down if it were a conspiracy to take over his empire. A hustler named Swayze James. Swayze was always on point with the hottest street happenings, and most of the time, he was involved in the shit; but Swayze wouldn't be involved in the grimy plot to take Alonzo's money. Alonzo knew that was his man from the days of his come-up and they always had a mutual love and respect for one another. He quickly two-wayed his fellow hustler.

"Beep...Guess who my man?" Alonzo said in a jovial tone as if he were expected to never be heard from again. "Beep...Alonzo! Boy what's going on? Damn, I ain't heard from you in a minute. You still holdin' it down in B-more?"

"You know it. Listen Sway, I'm in town and I need to holla at you 'bout some personal shit real important. Can we meet?"

"You know it, playboy. Meet me at the pool hall on Bay and Targee in 'bout an hour. Bring some dough, too, so I can take it on the pool table."

"Shittt, boy, you know you could never fuck with me on them sticks. Cool, though, see you soon."

As Alonzo walked through the smoke-filled bar/pool hall, he noticed that the place hadn't changed since his last visit there. Traveling to the back of the place, he spotted Swayze racking a set of pool balls on the pool table.

"Lost again, huh?" Alonzo laughed as he gave his long time balla a hug.

"Naw, these balls are for you. You better watch 'cause you'll be racking all night," Sway said, selecting two number 20 cue sticks from the wall rack.

"Ain't got that kinda time, homey." Alonzo grabbed the pool stick and broke through the pool balls. One stripped ball and one solid ball went in opposite pockets of the table. "I got highs," Alonzo called out.

Banking the number 15 ball into the side right pocket, Alonzo walked towards his friend, "Nigga's got my family, Sway."

"Family?" Swayze stepped back as if Alonzo's words were toxic. "Somebody kidnapped your whole family? Who?"

"No, just my cousin, Kwame. But they might as well have. Shorty's my heart. We're all we got. That's why I need to holla at you. I wanna know if you heard anything in the streets 'bout niggas making major moves in the streets on taking over cities down south."

Swayze had the look of concentration on his face as if he was figuring the theory of relativity. Tapping his long index finger against his temple, Swayze suddenly smirked.

"Yeah, couple months ago I heard some cats talking about Elite's moving business down south. He said it was a lot of money down there for the taking and he was gonna send some of his most thorough soldiers down to check out the prospects. I've never met 'em, but they 'pose to be some real grimy cats from Brooklyn. Certified killas."

Alonzo seemed impervious to Swayze's round-a-bout way of warning him of the kidnappers. With his mind focused on rescuing his cousin, Rambo himself wasn't gangsta enough to stop Alonzo from getting Kwame back. Without taking his eye off the last stripped pool ball on the table as he shot, Alonzo asked, "Who's this Elite?"

The thirteen ball slowly crept into the corner right pocket of the pool table, setting Alonzo up real lovely for the eight ball in the corner left.

Sway impressively nodded his head. "Nice shot. I see you've gotten better. In answer to your question though, Elite's a major playa in the game on his way to being the next fuckin' King of New York. Seemed like he came outta nowhere a couple years ago and straight blew Brooklyn up. He's got the whole burrow on lock, son, and half of the Bronx, too. Boy's got straight "hustler appeal" and knows where the money's at. Willing to do anything to get it, too. Looks like you got a war on your hands, son, 'cause I don't see him backing down. You prepared?"

Finessing the eight ball into the right corner pocket, Alonzo looked up at Sway and smirked, "Always, nigga."

After another game and a couple more drinks, Alonzo said his goodbyes to Sway and prepared himself for the anticipated phone call. Stroking his Glock and staring at the suitcase full of his money, Alonzo fumed at how much he hated giving into cowards scheming on what he fought so long and hard to build. No matter what though, he had to stay focused and smart if getting his cousin back was to come off easy, safe and as planned. Alonzo knew anger had no place in situations such as this.

Nine thirty on the dot Alonzo's cell rang. Alonzo took a long, deep breath and answered.

"Where you at, nigga, it's that time," a voice jeered at Alonzo.

"I'm here. Staten Island. Let's get this shit over with." Alonzo clinched his teeth.

"We make the demands, bitch, got that! Now drive to Brooklyn and I'll call back in a half hour. Better be alone, too." The phone clicked.

Twenty minutes later, Alonzo arrived at a little coffee shop in Brooklyn. Stressed about the whole situation, he needed a little boost of caffeine to calm his nerves and sober him from his slight buzz. Alonzo ordered a black coffee and a chocolate donut as he waited to hear his next order of instructions from the cowards that had his nerves on edge. Staring at his platinum and diamond bezel Maurice Lacroft, Alonzo wondered if he was being sent on some kinda wild goose chase on a plot to murder him. What if Kwame was already dead? What if he was never kidnapped at all? Alonzo's head was swimming with all kinds of doubts and scenarios. He lackadaisically sipped his lukewarm coffee as the waitress slid the bill under his plate. Ten o'clock as anticipated, Alonzo's phone rang promptly.

"I'm in Brooklyn, man, let's do this!" Frustrated, Alonzo wasn't in the mood for more delays.

"Listen to me, nigga!" the voice jeered back at him, matching his frustrated tone. "Water Street, Smith Projects under the Brooklyn Bridge. Drop the money off behind the…"

Alonzo shouted disagreeably, "You'll get the money when I see my cousin alive!"

"Just get there, motherfucka! First court on Water Street. Be by your fuckin' self."

"You'll have your money, just make sure you got my…" the phone clicked loudly.

Alonzo slowly pulled the jet black Escalade into Simmons Court. Except for the 24" spinning rims glistening into the night, the lot was completely dark. Alonzo drove to the end of the court and parked, leaving his lights on. Grabbing his twin Glocks, he scoured the lot from beginning to end; the possibility of an ambush strongly crossed his mind in a situation like this. Alonzo's cell rang.

"Turn your motherfuckin' lights out, nigga and get out the truck," a raspy voice whispered on the line.

Alonzo grabbed the suitcase full of money and complied. At a distance he saw a silhouette of a body motioning him with a hand gesture to walk straight ahead. Feeling the handle of his Glock with his right hand, Alonzo slowly approached the figure. He got within ten feet of the shadow in all black.

"Stop right there, nigga. Throw me the case and put your motherfuckin' hands over your head!" the voice commanded.

"Let me see him, then you'll get the money," Alonzo said, straining to keep calm.

"Bring this motherfucka out!" The man motioned to someone behind the building he stood beside. Kwame staggered from behind the building wall. Though he was unable to see him clearly, Alonzo could see that Kwame had been seriously fucked up and would be in need of medical attention. Alonzo just hoped it wasn't too late.

"A'ight, you seen him, now throw the loot."

Alonzo slid the black briefcase within a foot of the stranger. The dark figure retrieved the case and slowly flipped up the latches. He slowly lifted the case open.

"Kwame, duck!" Alonzo shouted as a cloud of thick, choking smoke rose from the suitcase into the stranger's face. Reaching for his twin Glocks, Alonzo simultaneously shot both guns into the cloud of smoke, lighting up the pitch-black night. Alonzo ran into the cloud of smoke scooping Kwame onto his shoulders and ran towards the Escalade.

Seconds later, the slain kidnapper's crew emerged from the front of the project building in response to the shots breaking the silence of the night. They were instantly met by a mirage of bullets spitting out the muzzle of a fully loaded Mack-10. Reap seemed to emerge outta nowhere and was now lying down anything that crossed his path. By the time the smoke cleared and Reap took his finger off the Mack-10's trigger, eight bodies laid expired on the project's asphalt. Reap slowly backed away towards the truck, still aiming the weapon. He disappeared into the backseat of the Escalade.

"Always coming through like the motherfuckin' Marc Train!" Alonzo looked back over the seat at his assassin and savior. Hurt and in shock, Kwame turned back and looked at Reap in total disbelief. What he just saw was truly some amazing shit.

Alonzo would never have dreamed of going out-of-town on such an important mission without his right-hand man. It had been Reap's idea of placing a pressure release smoke bomb into the suitcase to blast the fools. As a matter of fact, the whole plan was organized by Reap and executed to perfection. Reap was a certified killing technician and nobody did it better. He was well worth the $200,000 that was coming to him.

Kwame was seriously fucked up. Besides his severed index finger, he sustained various fractures and bruises way beyond inventory. His jaw was broken, making it nearly impossible to talk. Even if he could talk, he would decline with at least four teeth missing from his once flawless smile. Judging by the way Kwame was holing his sides, Alonzo suspected that his ribs were cracked and he might be bleeding internally. Alonzo immediately drove Kwame to the local hospital, hoping his injuries weren't life threatening.

Alonzo's and Reap's business wasn't completely finished in New York. Through Swayze, Alonzo learned that Elite had a very important function to attend at an elegant establishment in Downtown Manhattan. Neither Alonzo nor Reap knew what Elite looked like. They wouldn't have to. They only needed to know that he would be at the function tonight. His car wouldn't be that hard to spot either; a midnight blue 760 BMW Li with New York tags that said "ELITE" would be a dead give-a-way. Alonzo sped over the bridge towards Manhattan, hoping not to miss his appointment with his new found foe.

The Marriott Hotel on 46th and Broadway was a very plush establishment indeed. With rotating floors and a panoramic view of beautiful Manhattan, it was truly a place where big-timers came to unwind and enjoy the spoils of wealth. As Alonzo pulled up to the establishment, he was quite impressed with its accommodations. However, he thought with beefed up security and Valets throughout the premises, it might be hard for him to accomplish his mission. Nevertheless, he had the Grim Reaper on his team and that was nuff said. Reap always accomplished the mission and never slipped.

Alonzo circled the block and let Reap out the truck behind the hotel. They made plans to rendezvous back there in approximately an hour. That's how long Reap estimated it would take him to handle his business. Reap was a professional, so doing the job wasn't a problem, getting in and out undetected might be.

Exactly one hour later as planned, Alonzo drove back to the spot where he previously dropped off Reap. Reap casually entered the Escalade as if he was routinely being picked up Monday morning for work. Alonzo didn't have to ask a thing. Judging by the rarely seen smirk on Reap's face, he knew the deed was done. All was left to do now was to wait. As Alonzo circled the block, Reap playfully fondled the remote device between his fingers, still keeping the same devilish smirk on his face.

Inside the hotel, Elite was wrapping up his evening. It had been a good, joyous night of eating, drinking and partying with all of the major playas in the tri-state area and now Elite was planning to turn in early in anticipation of his wife's arrival from out of town tomorrow. He missed her extremely, but was use to her frequent business trips out of town. They had a mutual understanding, they both worked hard and played even harder.

Alonzo and Reap staked out at a secluded spot across the street from the hotel for what seemed like hours. Reap maintained constant watch over the hotel through high-powered binoculars, while Alonzo dosed in and out of la-la land from boredom. Alonzo was suddenly awakened from his nod.

"Get up, man, it's time," Reap said in his usual emotionless tone.

"He's coming?" Alonzo sprung up in anticipation.

"Yeah, the valet just brought his ride out front and he's about to get in. It's showtime, motherfucka!"

"Let me see." Alonzo took the binoculars from Reap and focused in close on his never seen, but sure to be, next victim. Squinting his eyes, he examined the face of the man entering the BMW. It couldn't be. But in his heart he knew who it was. It had been a long time, but he had seen that man's face many times before. Then he thought to himself…"Elite…Eric Little…My man Eric."

Alonzo was interrupted from his thoughts. "Is he in the car, Zo?" Reap asked impatiently.

In a low tone of voice, Alonzo answered, "Yeah." Then, getting a sudden grip on reality, Alonzo yelled out, "Reap, no!!!"

An earth-shattering *Ka-Boom* flooded throughout the streets, followed by frantic screams and screeching cars. It was too late. Reap wasted no time in pressing the detonator button on the remote and setting the BMW sky high in a blast full of flames. The shit happened instantaneously.

Alonzo was temporarily paralyzed. All he could think about was he had just killed his best friend. His Ace. They had come into the game together and now he had just taken Eric out. "Why Eric? Why you have to be the King of New York?"

Alonzo's mind was running a hundred miles an hour. He was once again interrupted from his thoughts.

"Come the fuck on, nigga! Don't you hear them sirens?"

Reap scrambled towards the Escalade. Reality suddenly sunk in Alonzo's head. He had to get Kwame and get the fuck outta town. He had now accomplished everything he had set out to do, so why did he feel so bad?

CHAPTER NINE: DEATH OF A SUPERSTAR

She impatiently stared at the ceiling in anticipation, waiting for her nightly ritual to come to an end. For three long months now, she bit her tongue, swallowed her pride, and kept her sanity through this whole ordeal, but now she was at her wit's end. As he mounted her for what she hoped would be his final climax for the evening, she tried long and hard to forget about her aching past that's haunted her for so many years. She tried to think of only pleasant thoughts, like that of her handsome son and the lavish life she was able to provide for him thus far. To no avail, the hideous images kept appearing over and over again in her head.

"Who's your daddy, girl, you sweet, young sexy bitch, you? Who's your daddy!"

"Owww! Daddy, please stop, you're hurting me! I can't take it anymore, stop!"

"Shut up, you nasty bitch! You wanna act grown, I'm gonna treat you like you're grown. Now stop swirming and take it!"

"I can't take it, I can't take it, get off of me…"

She began to swing uncontrollably at the man straddled over her.

"Damn, what the fuck is your problem, girl, I'm not raping you!" he said, shielding his face from the forceful and frequent blows he was abruptly receiving. "Calm down, it's me, baby, D-Coy. I'm not hurting you. It's okay."

Struggling to catch her breath, her eyes slowly began to focus on the image before her. It was sympathetic and understanding, far from the demon that appeared before her just seconds earlier. Judging by his demeanor, it was evident that it had happened again. One in a long series of uncontrollable and unpredictable blackouts.

"I'm sorry, baby," she said with a sudden display of innocence and compassion. He showed up again in my mind. I tried to fight it, but I just couldn't. I'm so sorry, let me make it up to you."

"Forget it, girl. When you're gonna realize I'm not him? I'm not that abusive boyfriend you just escaped from. I love you, girl. I'm not here to hurt you. I'm only here to make our life better and possibly take you as my queen in marriage. You gotta trust completely in me, baby, or this'll never work. Anyways, get some rest. We have a big day ahead of us tomorrow and I want you to be right. After all, it's not every day a man gets celebrated in his country. Everything must be right." He gently kissed her forehead and massaged her temples, calming her into a deep sleep.

It was the perfect afternoon to party in Kingston, Jamaica. The night was cool, the women were hot and the money was plentiful. The smooth, Caribbean sounds of the local live band filled the air along with thick clouds of smoke, compliments of Jamaica's best weed. The streets were filled with carefree tourist and wild locals partying like the world was gonna end tomorrow. It was a fantastic festival full of good food and good times. The guest of honor for tonight was no other than Devon McCoy, a.k.a. D-Coy, Kingston's most successful and most notorious Kingpin. Over the last few years, D-Coy's money paid for the renovation of fallen, grief-stricken neighborhoods and brought back a sense of hope to a once doomed community. D-Coy helped construct recreation centers and playgrounds throughout Kingston's neighborhoods, given less fortunate kids other options than robbing and stealing. D-Coy wasn't seen as a drug dealer in the community's eyes, but a hero that came to give them prosperity. He definitely deserved his honor.

D-Coy rode through the congested streets perched up high upon the seat of the convertible stretch Benz he was so lavishly being chauffeured in. As he looked around at all of his adoring fans, D-Coy couldn't help but to smile like a Cheshire Cat at all the good work he had done for his community. Though D-Coy had also been responsible for most of the bloodshed in Kingston, he reasoned that he was "divinely blessed" and anyone that stood in his way was the devil and deserved to die. He began to lift his arms like he was being resurrected as hundreds of spectators cheered his arrival.

"Yes, yes…I love you all," D-Coy exclaimed, now blowing smoke kisses at the crowd from his freshly rolled blunt. "Big up to Kingston, Big up to Jam…"

Blam…Blam…Blam

The crowd disbursed as multiple gun shots rang out through the air. D-Coy fell from his Godly stance as bullets riddled his body from top to bottom, giving him the appearance of a victim of an epileptic seizure. The chauffeur slumped in his seat from a bullet wound to the temple as the stretch Benz accelerated forward into a crowd of frantic patrons. It's progress ceased as it slammed into the newly constructed brick wall that encased the new recreation center that was being christened at the end of the days events. Police flooded the streets trying to restore order to the chaos that was now growing more and more out of control by the minute. A crowd gathered around D-Coy's lifeless body as if a national monument had been destroyed. He had been the savior of their neighborhoods. The sole provider for the promise of a better tomorrow for their impoverished economy. What were they to do now? A woman frantically made her way through the crowd towards D-Coy's bleeding corpse. She was of a slender build with honey blonde shoulder length hair and what would appear to be a fairly attractive face had it not been for the heavily swollen eyes and mournful disposition. She stared in disbelief as her husband lay tragically exposed on the street like common road kill.

"Devon, Devon baby, what happened! Wake up, baby, Devon!"

The woman fell down and clinched D-Coy's slain body for dear life. Eventually, she was restrained by police in order to secure the area for forensics and criminal investigations. Kicking, screaming and crying, police dragged the woman through the streets without compassion. As soon as she was able to compose her emotions, police Detective Patrick Stevens gave her his card to call in case she needed further assistance or had any clue who might have done this to her husband.

Detective Patrick Stevens was a dark, bald, rather robust man in his mid thirties. He had a noticeably long scar on the left side of his face, directly under his eye, that gave him an intimidating look to all that didn't know him. Though he stood 6'5", 300 pounds, Detective Stevens was a gentle giant. He was a native of Kingston that was employed with the police department for thirteen years. Throughout his career, Stevens had seen more of his share of senseless, brutal murders, most of which involved the victim whose murder he was now investigating. This murder struck him particularly odd though. Why would anyone in their right mind kill Devon McCoy. He was a legend in Kingston, like Nikki Barnes was in Harlem. One had to know that killing D-Coy was like committing suicide. It would be only a matter of time before his band of killas go on a head hunt to find whoever did this to their savior. D-Coy kept a lot of niggas fed over his rule of Kingston, and because of that, he had a lot of devoted workers. Detective Stevens knew that this wouldn't be the end of the bloodshed. He stroked his salt and pepper colored goatee in concentration as he watched the coroner load the body into the wagon to go to the mortuary.

CHAPTER TEN: THE DEADLY DIME

She stood 5 feet, 9 inches tall (6feet even in heels) and had the sexiest green eyes you ever saw on a woman. Her hair was jet black, healthy and flawless, flowing to the middle of her back whenever she wore it out, putting you in the mind of a young Jayne Kennedy back in the day when she played in Penitentiary. Her walk was exquisite, having a certain mystique about it that left all who witnessed it in aw. Her body was like a brick house, stacked with curves a Corvette couldn't handle. It should have been against the law for one woman to be so beautiful, but as beautiful as she was, she could be just as deadly.

When she walked into the gun shop, she knew exactly what she came to get. There wasn't any indecisive perusing or girlish bashfulness that you would find in most females in shopping for an item as powerful as a gun. She had complete confidence as she stepped towards the weapons clerk's counter to make her selection. "May I see the Glock 23 you have on display, please?"

The clerk obliged her. He stood in amazement as he watched the Angel before him lift and inspect the weapon. She maintained a firm grip on the weapon, then got into a shooter's stance so perfect that only a professional shooter would know how to position himself into. As she positioned her hand higher on the back-strap for a better sight alignment, the clerk knew that she was purchasing this weapon for more than protection; he knew that guns were her profession.

"I'll take one with adjustable sights," she said, reaching for her platinum Mastercard inside her Chanel bag that conveniently matched the Chanel outfit and shoes she wore so well.

"Yes, ma'am, anything else?" the clerk said anxiously as if he were a servant awaiting a command from his queen.

"A box of hollow tips, also," she added, flashing the clerk a smile, amused by his eagerness.

Reap stood at a separate counter of the shop pretending to be interested in a Remington 12-gauge shotgun, all the while concentration on the sexiness of the woman standing across from him. In recent years, he hardly ever conversed with anyone, much less a total stranger, being that he adapted an alter personality. Now he found himself searching for a cleaver word to say to the magnificent woman that had taken his breath away. Unrehearsed, he approached.

"Try not to hurt yourself," Reap blurted out for lack of a better pick-up line.

The woman rolled her eyes in irritation. "Don't worry, I'm a big girl."

"What I mean is, that's a lot of power for most females to handle. You should start off small for your first piece."

Unable to hold back her irritation anymore, the woman lashed out, "That's some arrogant bullshit to say. For your information, I'm not like most females. Furthermore, this piece completes my Glock collection. I have .9s and .45s and handle all of them well, probably better than your cocky ass. So the next time you wanna hand out advice, I suggest you don't judge a book by it's cover." The woman began to look Reap up and down.

"Damn, shorty, you some kinda scorned man killer?" Reap retaliated.

"Whatever!" The woman said, rolling her eyes and twisting her hips to exit the shop in frustration. "Asshole!" she murmured through her teeth.

Reap stared in total lust as he watched the angry woman's ass jiggle so perfectly as she stormed out the shop door. "Wait a minute, shorty." Reap ran to the shop door to cut off her exit. "We got off on the wrong foot. I mean no disrespect. I'm Reap," he said, extending his hand to the woman.

"Thai," she said, hesitantly accepting his hand, simultaneously blowing out air in an effort to relieve her irritation with him. "Next time if you wanna run game on me, try being more smooth and less arrogant.

"Point taken," Reap said with a gentle smile. "So, you collect guns, huh? How long?"

"About five years now. I have a fascination with big, black, powerful weapons," Thai said with a flirtatious grin, examining Reap's 6'3", chiseled muscular frame from top to bottom. Though he had just irritated her thoroughly, she couldn't deny that Reap was sexy with a body that screamed for her attention.

"Can you handle them, though?" Reap returned the flirtatious smirk.

"You can find out. I know a range in Westminster. Bring

your favorite piece tomorrow and save the shit talking for the targets. You down?" Thai asked, writing her phone number on the back of a matchbook she retrieved from her bag.

"Cool," Reap fought hard to hold back his enthusiasm. "It's a date."

"No, it's a competition," Thai said, sliding into a champagne-colored 745i. "Don't get it twisted." The BMW took off down the street.

It had been years since Reap had gone out with a woman. With his profession, he hadn't the personality or patience to tolerate a woman and up to now hadn't seen one that sparked his interest. Since Chay, Reap had limited his relationships with women to cheap one night stands or wild freak escapades whenever Alonzo would have one of his infamous parties. In Reap's mind, women were trouble and a distraction to all he hoped to achieve in his line of work. He couldn't have someone knowing what he did for a living. After all, women don't get angry, they get even, and that left the window open for his downfall. Reap knew he would have to kill a woman if he ever broke her heart and that was a road he was not willing to travel. However, it was something about the woman he just met that made him forget about all of that.

When Reap arrived on the range, Thai was already there busting rounds off at a paper target down-range with a black silhouette. He instantly thought that even in camouflage BDU's, she was still one of the most captivating woman he ever laid eyes on.

"You're late," Thai said, simultaneously squeezing off six rounds from the sweet Glock she bought yesterday.

"Better late than never," Reap responded, analyzing her shots. Still focusing on her target, Thai reloaded another clip. "Let's see what you got."

From 25 yards away, Reap and Thai fired weapons at the paper targets downrange. After firing three full clip, the two looked at each other. Both responded, "Not bad."

All of Reap's shots landed center mast as always. Though he had clearly won the competition, Thai was one of the best shooters he ever saw, male or female. He had only beaten her by a shot or two. After shooting off a few more boxes of ammunition, they decided to call it a day.

"Wanna grab a bite to eat, black widow?" Reap said as he watched Thai meticulously breakdown her weapon for cleaning.

"Sure, why not? After showing me up out here, the least you could do is buy me dinner. If I didn't know any better, I'd think you did this for a living."

Reap's heart rate shot up. "Naw, shorty, just a long-time hobby of mines."

"If you call shooting mothafuckas a hobby." Thai smiled and cleverly changed the subject. "I know a nice little restaurant down the street. Follow me there."

Reap and Thai drove to the restaurant and conversed for two hours over a plate of rotisserie chicken, mashed potatoes, mixed vegetables and corn bread. After the meal, Thai and Reap decided they wanted to go to the movies. "Follow me home, big boy, so I can change. Can't be seen in public with this G.I. Jane shit on," Thai said, winking at Reap.

As Reap followed behind Thai, he wondered how the fuck she even knew or even had an idea about what he did for a living. Though he said nothing to her about it over dinner, the curiosity was killing him ever since she first jokingly mentioned it at the range. How could she possibly know he was a killer-for-hire just from his shooting skills? Something didn't feel quite right in this scenario to him. Though "set up" was on his mind the entire time on the journey to her house, Reap continued to follow the BMW towards the upscale area of Randallstown. If she was "Fed-Time" he would soon find out and put an end to any case she planned to bring up on him or Alonzo. Reap promptly loaded a fresh clip in his 9mm Beretta as he followed Thai into her driveway.

Thai's house looked like a mini-mansion, equipped with large stained glass windows and life-sized statues adorning the front entrance of the house. It sat on a half acre of land, void of any neighboring houses. It looked like something that should've been on "MTV Cribs" or some shit like that. If Thai was living like that, she was a Balla fo' real. If this was a front, the Feds spared no expense in trying to pinch his black ass. She was the finest bitch he ever saw, with a tight whip and a mean crib. Too extravagant to be an agent, still Reap was skeptical. He put the 9mm in the small of his back as he exited the truck.

"Nice house. You didn't say we were breaking and entering before the movie," Reap joked, trying to ease his nerves.

"Ha-Ha…everybody's a comedian. Bring your silly self on in before I change my mind."

Thai opened the door to what looked like a palace inside. The house was enormous and immaculate, with every piece of furnishing in its place. The walls were aligned with various pieces of African artwork that gave the house an exotic appeal. The atmosphere was amazing, yet subtle enough that anyone could easily make their self at home upon entrance.

Reap entered the house with caution, scanning every corner of the house as he proceeded through the door. It had evolved into his nature to be always on point, especially when entering a place for the first time; he always felt that you never know when a set-up might take place. Reap seen a lot of supposed-to-be killers go down in conspiracies set-up by beautiful women. He wasn't having it.

Reap gripped the handle of his Beretta as he followed Thai to the west-wing of the house. Thai sensed Reap's uneasiness. In an effort to make him more at ease, she sat him on a plush, Italian made sofa that seemed to accent the already magnificent living room. Reap sunk into the sofa like quicksand. It was the most comfortable couch he had ever had the privilege to sit on. In a soft, seductive, soothing tone, Thai whispered, "Relax."

Thai began to remove her BDU top, exposing her perfectly formed abs. Slowly she lifted her tee shirt, exposing her firm, beautifully rounded, butterscotch breast, encased in a lavender Victoria's Secret bra. As she lifted her arms over her head to release the shirt, she threw her head back in ecstasy, reminiscent of a soft porn scene. Thai then proceeded to remove her BDU trousers. The pants freed themselves, exposing Thai's shapely hips and thick, smooth thighs. As the pants fell to the floor, Thai seductively stepped out of each leg, kicking the pants out of her way.

"I don't know what line of work you're in, Reap, but you seem tense. As you can see, Mr. Reap, I have no weapons or wires, so you can relax." Stretching her arms to the side, Thai turned around giving Reap a full view of her backside.

The only weapon Reap saw was the plump ass cheeks peeking through Thai's matching lace Victoria's Secret panties. At this point, Reap wasn't even thinking about looking for a wire or reaching for his gun—at least not the kind with bullets. He closed his eyes in ecstasy and moaned, "Yes, I see."

"Would you like to feel also?" Thai teased, looking back over her shoulder. "We women have a lot of hiding places."

"I'd better give you a pat-down then." Reap rose from the sofa, lightly touching Thai's shoulder. He softly caressed her arms as he moved his frisk to her upper torso. Reap gently cupped her soft supple breast. Instantaneously, he softly kissed the nape of her neck, forgetting the purpose of what he was doing. He hadn't felt this aroused since Chay. Reap felt a rush of passion throughout his entire body. It felt powerful and controlling, as if fire was burning his soul. Without asking, Reap explored every curve and crevice of Thai's superb body. This was a feeling he didn't ever want to leave him.

Thai responded to Reap's passion. In anticipation, she undressed him and ran her hands over his tight, muscular frame. She kissed down his chest as she ventured below to send satisfaction to her awaiting new lover. Reap's body was that of a Nubian God to her, worthy to be made love to nice and slow. Like a naughty schoolgirl, Thai gently touched and teased Reap to the point of an erotic explosion, sending him to a new height of arousal he had never reached before. Then, without warning, Thai stopped. She suddenly stood up, took Reap's hand and led him up the elegant spiral stairway leading to her bedroom. This was an area of the house few men visited. Thai's bedroom was only reserved for the privileged and, at this point, Reap had earned the privilege to be treated special simply because he was so sexy and had her boiling over. She seductively laid Reap down on the queen-sized canopy and continued her arousal.

The two made love beautifully, as if fate commanded their bodies to unite. Though it was spontaneous and hasty, this was more than a one night stand in both the lover's minds, this was their destiny. With every stroke, Reap was more and more convinced that it was something about this woman that made her the one. It was like he suddenly forgot his "killer instinct" and replaced it with soft feelings of warmth and desire, shit he was not allowed to feel. Making his final approach to climax, Reap rolled off Thai in exhaustion. This escapade he just experienced had been more energetic and fulfilling than any workout he ever had.

Reap and Thai skipped the movies, laid and talked until the wee hours of the morning. Reap told her nothing of his profession, but shared with her his plans and goals for the future. Thai told Reap of her humble beginnings. She was originally from the projects of Detroit, an ex-bad girl who ran with a few gangs and even organized her own all female gang. That was how her skills with the iron developed. Out of necessity and a near death experience, she left Detroit to live with her stable aunt and uncle in uptown New York. Through patience, effort, care, love and money, Thai's new family transformed her life. They helped her stay out of trouble, graduate high school and get accepted into St. John's college. She was now a top executive in a real estate firm in Maryland. That explained the phat crib and whip. Despite changing her life for the better, Thai was still a bad-girl for life and had a love for thugs. It was something about a man that packed heat and wasn't afraid to bang it anywhere or on anybody that drove her absolutely wild. To her, for some unknown reason, Reap had the instinct of a no-nonsense killer. Yet, if tapped into, had the heart of a perfect Angel.

CHAPTER ELEVEN:
THE UNVEILING

Detective Stevens was having a bad morning. For starters, he had burned his toast, spilled his coffee, cut his self shaving and needed a jump start to his car battery because he had left his lights on all night. To make matters worse, when he arrived in his office, he had a shit load of paperwork to finish from the preceding day. Detective Stevens rubbed his head in frustration just wondering how the rest of his day was going to turn out.

It had been almost two months and Stevens still hadn't received any intelligence in solving Devon McCoy's murder. One would think that a murder that took place on the street in broad daylight, with at least three hundred witnesses would be solved by now, or at least, produce a suspect, but it hadn't. He was no closer to solving the murder from the day it happened. Detective Stevens took a sip of his coffee and attempted to shift through the papers on his desk. His cell phone rang, instantly irritating him. It was too early for him to be bothered by anything this morning. Hesitantly, he answered.

"Homicide, Detective Stevens, how may I help you?"

"Yes, Mr. Stevens, this is Patricia McCoy, D-Coy's wife.

Detective Stevens day instantly got worse. He remembered telling Mrs. McCoy to call him if she needed anything, how could he now have nothing to help her with? Nevertheless, in his most professional voice, he spoke. "Oh, hello Mrs. Stevens, how can I help you.

"Well, the day Devon was killed, you gave me your card to call you if I had a clue about who may have been responsible for my husband's murder. I think I may have found something to help you."

Detective Stevens almost dropped the phone in excitement. He had forgotten he told Mrs. McCoy to call if she had a clue in the case. He thought she was calling to get information, but she was giving it. This was shaping up to be a good day after all. "Well, okay Mrs. McCoy, do you feel comfortable about talking over the phone or do you want…"

"Yes I wanna come down to the station," Mrs. McCoy interrupted Stevens mid-sentence. "I have some pictures you need to see."

"Okay, Mrs. McCoy, see you in about an hour."

Detective Stevens quickly gathered up the jumbled papers on his desk and threw them in the nearest cabinet he could find. He then began to tidy up his office, so it would have the appearance of a detective's office instead of a security guard shack. D-Coy's murder was the biggest murder Kingston had in years and now he might be the one to solve it. This would skyrocket his career. Detective Stevens got the tape recorder prepared to tape any statements Mrs. McCoy was prepared to give.

Exactly one hour, Mrs. McCoy knocked on Detective Stevens office door. With pleasure in his voice, Detective Stevens answered, "Come in."

Mrs. McCoy entered the office. She was a very attractive woman. Her Hershey chocolate brown completion seemed to brighten the room as soon as she walked in. Her hair was long and silky, colored black this time, and styled in a feathered wrap. She was dressed conservatively in a black Dolce and Gabana pants suit, accented by a peach collared Dolce and Gabana buttoned blouse. Her physique was her best feature. Slender in build and toned to perfection, it was obvious that Patricia McCoy had done some modeling at some point in her life. Walking over to Detective Stevens desk, she spoke in a sexy Jamaican accent, "Hello Detective."

"Hello yourself," Detective Stevens was a little thrown back by Mrs. McCoy's beauty. When he first saw her, she was distraught over her husband's death, so she wasn't nearly as intriguing as she was now. Getting a hold of himself, he gently stated, "So, what do you have for me?"

Mrs. McCoy laid a brown manila envelope on his desk. "Pictures. Of Devon and this woman. I know Devon wasn't faithful to me, he had many mistress's. I expected that, Devon was a man of prestige and many women wanted him. I never said anything 'cause Devon always kept me first. However, there was something that didn't sit right with me about this woman. Devon spent a lot of time with her and flaunted her around as his new wife. The funny thing is that since Devon's murder, no one has seen head or tales of this woman. She didn't even come to his funeral. I feel that she might know something about or have something to do with D-Coy's murder. I just found these pictures when I was going through D-Coy's things the other day. I just thought you could use them."

Detective Stevens opened the envelope, took out the pictures and perused through them. There were nine pictures of Devon and a brown-completed woman with deep green eyes. They appeared to be very much in love with each other as far as the pictures shown, hugged up and kissing on practically every other picture. The detective rubbed his chin and shifted through each picture again carefully. " These might be helpful to me Mrs. McCoy, thank you. Is there any more information you have for me?"

"Yes, right before Devon's parade, he came home with scratches and bruises on his face, like he was fighting, but with a female. When I asked him what happened, he just snapped at me and told me to mind my business. Then he got a bag and stormed out of the house. That was the last time I saw him alive."

"Thanks, Mrs. McCoy, I promise you I'll investigate these pictures as hard as I can and bring some closure to your life. I'll call you as soon as I get a break in the case."

"Good. I pray that you find this woman Detective and bring her to justice. Matter of fact, bring her to me. She took my Devon, I know she did." Mrs. McCoy broke down in tears and walked swiftly out of the office without saying goodbye. "I'll do my best Mrs. McCoy," Detective Stevens yelled out as she stormed away.

Detective Stevens started his investigation by blowing up a picture of the woman's face and faxing it to every police precinct in Jamaica along with a statement saying that she is a suspect in Devon "D-Coy" McCoy's murder. He also was authorized to offer a $10,000 reward to anyone knowing information about her whereabouts. He also faxed some of the wanted pictures to some police precincts stateside just in case she fled the island. Detective Stevens closed his eyes and silently prayed for the best.

CHAPTER TWELVE:
THUG CONFESSIONS

One again, the lovemaking had been so intense that Reap hadn't heard his two-way.

Beep…"Reap you there? Where you at man, I need to talk to you…Reap!"

It had been like this for the past two months. Reap was so into his new love affair that his contact with Alonzo, or anybody else for that matter, had been nearly in existence. Through candlelight dinners, deep conversations and erotic escapades, Thai had him open. She had managed to do in two months what no other male or female could do in twelve years…Make Reap weak.

Exhausted, Reap answered the call. "What's up man?"
"You tell me." The frustration in Alonzo's voice was more than evident. "I've been trying to get in contact with you for the last two days man, why didn't you hit me back?"

"My bad, Zo, just been busy, you know." Reap playfully glanced at Thai and winked his eye. "What's so important?"

"I got something to tell you about that bitch you been spending so much time around."

"Watch your fuckin' mouth, man, I'm not gonna tell you that again. Now what is it?" Reap said, fuming at what Alonzo had just called Thai. Thai looked up at Reap in disbelief.

"Look, my bad man, but it's something real important you need to know about her but I can't talk about it over the phone, you know the code. Meet me at the crib in a half if you're not too busy. You need to know this Reap."

"On my way." Reap sighed as he hung up the call. "Gotta take care of business baby, be back later on tonight."

"I don't know what's wrong with your friend, but he better watch who he's calling a Bitch; I don't play that shit; Anyway, I'll be waiting for you, sweetie, see you then." Thai grabbed Reap by the neck and gave him a deep, hot passionate kiss that almost had him taking back off his clothes and forgetting about what Alonzo had to tell him about her. "Just a little some'in to take with you," Thai said, passionately staring into Reap's eyes.

"Keep that up and I'll have to take some more. Damn, the things you do to me girl, got me going crazy. Let me get outta here while I still can." Reap slid his jacket over his broad shoulders and left out the door.

Though he said it in a joking way, Reap was serious. Thai really had him going crazy. It had always been M.O.B. with Reap—Money Over Bitches. That was his motto and words to live by, but for some reason he was finding it harder and harder to leave her side. This was some real sucker shit. Reap needed a quick reality check. He always told himself that if he wanted to succeed in this murder game, there couldn't be no distractions. Although he didn't want to do it, Reap knew he would have to break it off with her regardless of what Alonzo told him about her. He would let her down easy tonight.

Thai laid in the bed filled with satisfaction. She never thought that she would be so into a Bounty Hunter. Up until this point, she had been exclusively attracted to corporate CEO's and major money-getters. Thai was far from a gold-digger though, she just wanted a man to be on the same level she was on. With Reap, it didn't matter though. Over the past two months, she had been so emotionally, mentally and sexually satisfied with him that his financial status had no real bearing. What was Reap talking about, she was the one that was really going crazy. As Thai began to get deeper and deeper in thoughts of Reap, she knew that she had to finally tell him the truth, she would tell him tonight.

Reap knocked on Alonzo's door heavily, in anticipation of Alonzo's news. Alonzo slowly opened the door.

"Good, you made it. I won't keep you waiting man, look." Alonzo handed Reap a picture of Thai with a wanted caption printed under her picture. It further said that she was wanted as a suspect in a murder that occurred in Kingston, Jamaica. "I got this out of the post office today. They had it posted with all the other wanted pictures. I know I only seen her briefly once Reap, but that's Thai. Those eyes are unforgettable. You've got to drop her Reap, we don't need that kind of extra heat on us, shit, we're hot enough from this New York shit."

"Yeah that's her alright," Reap said, dropping his head in disappointment but trying to stay strong. I'll cut her off tonight. Thanks, man, I know I was slipping for a minute, but I'm back."

"That's good to know Reap. You're gonna be alright?"

"Yeah, I'm cool. I just need to clear my head awhile. Holla at you tomorrow." Reap left out the door in a hurry.

Reap pulled into Thai's driveway midnight on the nose. Finding out the news of Thai being on the run fucked up his head beyond belief. On top of that he still knew that he was falling dangerously in love with her and that was unacceptable. He had to stay focused and emotion-free in the game he was in. He sat in his truck for twenty more minutes trying to get his words right. Finally, Reap slowly exited the truck and proceeded to Thai's door. Before he could knock, Thai opened the door.

"Hey, baby," Thai said, trying not to send Reap the vibe that something was on her mind.

Reap stared at her with disappointment. "Explain this!" Reap held the wanted picture in front of Thai's eyes.

Thai's heart-rate instantly shot through the roof. "Where…Where did…"

"Never mind where I got it, explain it!" Reap had a blank look on his face.

Thai momentarily was speechless. It was news to her that she was wanted for anything. Hesitantly, she spoke. "He was a molester and a murderer. He molested and killed a little girl in Atlanta and went back to Jamaica to escape prosecution. I was contracted to go there to kill him."

"Contracted?" Reap was really confused now. "What you mean you were contracted?"

"I'm a contract killer Reap. I should have told you earlier but I didn't know how. It's not full-time, only when it's a hit I feel that needs to be done. That hit needed to be done."

Reap was devastated beyond words. After a long silence, he simply stated, "I'm out." He turned to walk out of the door.

"Reap wait. Just let me explain everything from the beginning and if you still feel you wanna leave then you're free to go. Please, baby, I really do love you."

"Shoot. I'm sure you're used to hearing that word, right?" Reap stepped back and listened to Thai's story.

Thai rolled her eyes at Reap and started from the beginning. Her birth name had been Thailand Smith. She had been the product of a broken family. Though both parents were in the home, Thai lived a very dysfunctional life. Her mother, Stephanie, was a manic depressant, who for years tried to live a normal life hooked on Percocet. Though she tried to be a good mother to Thai, half of the time she was too spaced out of her mind to show her any concern. The other half she spent wallowing in her own self misery and depression. Thai's father, Jerome, was just the opposite. He was self assured and confident. However, he was a chronic alcoholic that was regularly abusive. On any given night, he would stumble in the house stinking drunk and verbally abuse Stephanie until he passed out from his pathetic high. Other times, on not-so-lucky nights, he would smack her around from one end of the room to another until she begged him to stop. However, no matter how abusive Jerome was to Stepahie, it couldn't compare to the abuse he imposed on Thai. He damaged her in so many other ways. He had other ways of damaging her. Jerome had been secretly molesting Thai since the age of seven. He was an excellent manipulator, so he swore that if she ever told, he would kill her mother and she would be sent to live in foster homes, which at the time was worse than death to a seven year old. Then in his own twisted way, Jerome would comfort Thai with inappropriate kisses and embraces that would eventually lead to sex with his young daughter. For some reason, Thai represented beauty and innocence to him that he couldn't appreciate in no other form than sex.

Jerome handled Thai like an experienced woman, savagely damaging her anatomy and her spirits. Not knowing any better, Thai interpreted her father's incestuous lust as genuine love. No matter what pain he put her through, she was still "Daddy's little girl" and thought the world of her father. It would be a couple of years before she realized the injustice her father was really doing to her.

By the time Thai was eleven, she hated her father. Now, not only did she realize that Jerome was wrong in his nightly visits with her, she also was growing tired of seeing the pain and agony he was putting her mother through. Stephanie was now a full-fledged junkie. She graduated from depression medications to heroin in an effort to deal with her abusive husband. Now Stephanie was totally helpless to Thai. She had to deal with Jerome daily on her own. Thai began to be regularly absent from school because of her problems. Everyday she would ball up on her bed and cry her eyes out, wishing she could somehow disappear from there into a far-off fairy tale land where there were no "Evil Daddy's." Thai felt like she had no one to talk to, so almost all of her time was spent in her room. Her dolls and her imagination were her only friends.

It was two o' clock in the morning, and Jerome was on his nightly routine. He had quietly staggered into Thai's room and was now straddled on top of his sleeping daughter. Jerome began to kiss on Thai's tender neck while he gently fondled her young vagina. The more aroused he got, the harder he poked inside Thai, waking her up from her peaceful sleep. Jerome was so encased in his perverted actions that he hadn't noticed Thai reaching under her mattress. As he unleashed his manhood for penetration, he jumped up as young Thai screamed, "I can't take this shit no more!" Thai closed her eyes and swung the butcher's knife for dear-life. Not even knowing if she hit her target, she continued to swing, totally impervious to the blood that began to splatter on her face. By the time Thai stopped swinging and opened her eyes, Jerome laid backwards in a pool of blood, stabbed 32 times in various places in his body. Thai was speechless and in shock. She suddenly broke down in tears at the sight of her mother standing in the doorway.

Stephanie had a nervous breakdown after witnessing her husband's murder at the hand's of her daughter. She knew nothing of all the years of molestation of her precious daughter. All she knew was that she saw her only daughter murder her husband. She was ultimately admitted into a psychological center for long-time treatment. Thai lived her worse nightmare and was now a ward of the State of Michigan. The courts thought it would be too harsh a punishment to send her to Juvenile Detention in spite off all she been through, thus they tried to find alternative care for young Thai. Finding no family willing to take her in, the courts were forced to place Thai in foster care. To Thai, that was the end of life as she knew it.

Everyone knew that a twelve year old kid with a murder-rap had no chance of being adopted, so Thai gave up hope. Throughout the years, she purposely did every destructive thing under the sun to get shipped from group home to group home. Thai was a certified menace, constantly running away and being arrested. She ran with a group of delinquent girls that shared her same story of hardship. They eventually formed an infamous gang known as BDB (Bad Destructive Bitches) with Thai as their ringleader. BDB became known for terrorizing the streets of Detroit.

During her run with BDB, Thai grew more cold and callous. It was nothing for her to shank another girl or a guy from a rival gang and think nothing of it. Thai was quite "nasty" with a blade. So nice in fact, a local drug dealer employed her to be his enforcer. Thai had the complete package to him; beauty, heart, and street knowledge.

Thai put in work as an enforcer. By the time she was twenty, she had slashed too many throats to take count. As her body count rose, so did her stock in "Murder for Hire." Thai was offered anywhere from $1,000 to $10,000 for hits. Thai quickly stepped up her weapon game from knives to firearms, where she became just as effective. She gained the reputation of getting the job done with beauty, grace and style.

Thai earned enough money from killing to invest in her own business. A real estate firm seemed like a good way to launder her hit money as well as make a fortune legitimately. Thai wasn't totally outta the murder game though, if the price was right, she would be more than happy to offer her services. And in the case of Devon McCoy, the price was definitely right along with the principle. There was no room for murdering child molesters in the world.

A tear rolled down Thai's eye as she wrapped up her life story to Reap. At a lost for words, Reap gently embraced Thai and held her tight in his bosom.

He finally said, "Baby, you could've told me. All this time you had me believing something else, you should've told me."

Reap thought how could he be mad at Thai for doing the same work he did. Yeah it was fucked up he had to find out this way, but if the shoe was on the other foot, he probably would've done the exact same thing. She was right, a motherfucka like D-Coy deserved to die, and if she could get paid handsomely to do it herself, then why not. His mind said leave the situation, but his heart said stay and support her through her struggle. He definitely had no right to judge her. Suddenly, Reap felt a sense of guilt in his heart. Against his better judgment, he solemnly told her, " I have something to tell you, too."

CHAPTER THIRTEEN:
THE MEETING

Alonzo packed his bags in anticipation of his business trip to Miami. The thought of making new money always excited Alonzo and made him impatient. He just hoped his new supplier would live up to what he was hyped up to be. Emilio Sanchez was a savvy young Columbian multimillionaire that made his fortune in drugs. He was the major supplier of drugs in the South and East coast, and was known for having the purest product at the most reasonable prices. For months, Alonzo and he played phone-tag, trying to set up a meeting between them, and finally now was the time. Alonzo just hoped everything would go well.

As Alonzo looked at his diamond Rolex, he wondered what was taking Reap and that bitch so long. Their departure time from the airport was 8:00a.m. and it was now 7:05. Alonzo hated being late for anything, much less a business opportunity, and his patience was growing thin. Why didn't Reap take his advice and drop that bitch anyway. Being on the run, she was too hot to be traveling with them. However, Reap insisted that they worked things out and everything was cool, whatever that meant. He also insisted that if he went, she went, and Alonzo definitely needed Reap to go. After all, he was his man and always came through more times than he could ever count. If it wasn't for him, Alonzo knew he would've been dead a long time ago. He would have to trust Reap's judgment. If he said she was cool, then that's what it was. Anyway, two killas had to be better than one. Alonzo just hoped they would hurry up.

Reap and Thai slowly pulled into Alonzo's driveway. Exiting the truck, Reap looked up at Alonzo and grinned, "Are we late?"

"We good man," Alonzo said, trying to hide his irritation. "Bring your bags over here."

Reap and Thai unloaded their bags from the truck and reloaded them into the Mercedes G-5 Wagon. Looking at Alonzo, Reap said, "You remember Thai?"

"Yeah we met before, how you doing Thai?" Alonzo asked nonchalantly.

"I'm fine," Thai stated, equally as unimpressed.

The three loaded into the G-5 and made their way to BWI International Airport. In his mind, Reap hoped that this would be more of a vacation trip for him than business, but in the drug world, you never know. At the airport, Thai looked around nervously and hoped that no one would recognize her with her wig and dark shades on. The last thing she wanted to do was get knocked off in an airport.

They arrived in sunny Miami by11:00a.m. After they checked into the Island Outpost, the luxury four-star, ocean front hotel they were staying in, Reap and Thai decided to take a stroll on the beach. Alonzo immediately went to the post office and checked his P.O. box for the guns he had pre-shipped to Miami. Airport security was too tough to try smuggling weapons by. As far as the kilos he planned to purchase from Emilio, he had plans for them, too. Emilio would charter a boat before their departure to arrive in Baltimore. Alonzo had workers on standby to meet the boat and handle the transaction. Everything would go smoothly. Retrieving the weapons from the box, Alonzo hoped that this trip wouldn't turn out to be like New York. The odds would be against them to beef with some real Columbians in unfamiliar territory. Deadly odds.

Reap and Thai played on the beach until nightfall, where they eventually made love. The moon over Miami was so full and perfect, they couldn't pass it up. This was a night indeed made for lovers. As the two bodies became one on the blissful beach, Reap now knew that this would be his final job for Alonzo. When they returned home, Reap would ask Thai to give up contract killing and marry him. They would move out of state, maybe somewhere down south, like the Carolinas. Either of which, Reap had more than enough money saved over the years for the both of them to be very happy. Reap could only hope that she would give up her life and accept his hand in marriage. As Reap held Thai's soft body in the moist sand, he thought to himself, "This must be some powerful pussy to make me give up my entire life.

The next afternoon, the meeting was underway. Alonzo, Reap and Thai sat in the midst of Emilio's ancient Villa awaiting his arrival. The whole scene reminded them of *Scarface*, when Tony met Frank. Emilio was truly a Drug Lord in every scene of the word, complete with his own army of dedicated thugs. Every room of the villa was guarded by two trigger happy looking henchman. Yet, Alonzo couldn't wait to seal the deal between them.

Emilio's entrance in the room was princely. He was of average height, with jet black, wavy hair. He sported a pencil-thin beard that made him look more like a model than a drug kingpin. His hands were freshly manicured, as if he hadn't worked a decent job in his life. Dipped in a crisp, crimson linen outfit, everyone sat in silence as Emilio greeted his guest.

"Hola, amigos. Como estas?"

"Muy bien, gracias," Alonzo said in his best Latin accent, standing to shake Emilio's hand.

"So finally we meet. Tell me, who are your friends?"

"Well, this is an associate of mines, Reap, and this is Thai, his fiancée." Alonzo cut his eyes at Thai as he said her name. Reap and Thai stood up in unison. "Please to meet you," the both of them said.

"As well. Tell me, will Mr. Reap be doing business with me as well."

"Naw, he's with me on vacation, compliments of me in celebration of his engagement."

"I see. Well, congratulations Reap, you have a very lovely fiancée. Shall we proceed with business, Alonzo?"

"That's why I'm here."

"Very well. Follow me. Your friends could stay here. We shall not be long," Emilio said, shooting a wink in Thai's direction.

Emilio and Alonzo proceeded down a long corridor towards another wing of the Villa. They were follow by two of Emilio's hefty henchmen. Reap wanted desperately to follow behind Alonzo, but didn't want to blow the deal. Instead, he and Thai stayed alert, listening for warning signs.

Twenty minutes later, Emilio and Alonzo returned, talking and laughing like two old Army buddies.

"I would like to invite you all back here tonight for a party, in celebration of me and Alonzo's partnership, and of course, your engagement, Mr. Reap." Emilio flashed Thai a friendly smile.

Before Reap and Thai could respond, Alonzo stated, "We accept. What time shall we be here?"

"Nine would be good. And, please, bring your appetites. My chefs are truly amazing."

"Will do. See you then."

As the three exited the villa, Reap pulled Alonzo to the side. "You sure you trust this cat, man, he seemed suspect to me. All this Rico Suave shit, I don't know, man, seems fake."

"Look, all I know is that I got two hundred keys of quality coke in route to B-more as we speak. That alone may quadruple my worth. I don't care if the mothafucka's Ricky Ricardo. He's gonna make me rich."

"A'ight, man, I hear you. But something about dude ain't right, I'm telling you."

"You worry too much, Reap, relax."

The three headed back to the hotel for some relaxation before the party. Miami was beautiful, but extremely hot and exhausting. The afternoon sun had drained them. The night was just as hot as the three headed for the party in the stretched Bentley limousine Emilio sent for them. All of them wished for the cooler, less humid weather of Baltimore. Nevertheless, they were enjoying themselves and were sure that they would have a great evening.

All eyes were on Thai as she entered the hall of the Villa. She was dressed in a sleeveless red Armani dress that hugged every curve of her vivacious body. Her hair was pinned up, accentuating the texture of her flawless face. Her deep green eyes seemed to glow in the dimness of the hall. Emilio spotted her and approached.

"Hola, glad you all could make it. Please, come to my table and dine with me."

"It would be our honor," Alonzo spoke out for the three.

They headed for Emilio's table located in the center of the hall. The room was filled with, what looked like, hundreds of people eating, drinking and dancing. Compared to this, all of Alonzo's parties looked like back yard barbeques. Alonzo, Reap and Thai ordered their dinner from the elegant menus placed on the table. Everything sounded delicious and the waiters were very delightful. They explained the Columbian dishes thoroughly.

Everything was delicious. After a few drinks and casual conversation, everyone was relaxed.

"Would I be out of order if I asked your fiancée to dance, Reap?" Emilio asked, smiling at Thai.

"It's up to her." Reap shrugged, giving Emilio a distant look. "Thai, may I?"

"Sure, why not." Thai stood and the two headed for the dance area.

Emilio and Thai salsaed to two fast-pace Latin grooves. Thai was as graceful as a swan, twisting and turning on time and rhythm. She loved Latin music. The third song was slow. Emilio closely embraced Thai without permission.

"May I?" Emilio asked.

"Just this one song and I'm going to sit down, I'm tired."

"Okay. You know, Thai, you are truly a beautiful woman." Emilio tightened his embrace on Thai's back.

"Thank you," Thai said, squirming to loosen Emilio's grip.

"I'm serious. In my country, a woman such as yourself would be worshipped. Thai, you are truly a treasure. I knew that from the moment I laid eyes on you. Darling, come live with me in my villa. I'm so intrigued by you. You have no business dealing with a man of Reap's caliber. I can make you a very rich woman."

"Let go of me right now and I'll chalk what you just asked me up as you being drunk. You hardly know me."

"I know your spirit. I want you, sweetheart." Emilio lowered his hand and squeezed a handful of Thai's apple ass.

Swiftly Thai reached in her cleavage and pulled out a butterfly knife she had been used to carrying since her juvenile days. She stuck the blade in Emilio's nostril. "Let go of me, bitch, before I jab this blade in your motherfuckin' skull."

Emilio's henchmen saw the drama and aimed at Thai with drawn .45s. Reap bolted from the table and placed a loaded .357 to Emilio's head.

"We can all die in this motherfucka tonight. How you want it, homey?" Reap said, with a look of death in his eyes.

Emilio shook his head no. The henchmen immediately withdrew their aim. "My bad, just a simple misunderstanding," Emilio said with a smile.

"What the fuck ever," Reap withdrew the gun. "Let's go."

Alonzo sat at the table confused by all that had just transpired. "Let's go!" Reap repeated loudly. The three exited the party with all eyes on them. The room was completely silent. The evening was over.

Reap, Thai and Alonzo flew back to Baltimore in silence. Though Alonzo briefly wanted to retract the deal with Emilio, the wheels were already in motion. He had just spent five million dollars on two hundred keys of quality pure coke that was headed to Fells Point. Reap would just have to forgive him. They been through tougher times.

CHAPTER FOURTEEN: MO' MONEY, MO' PROBLEMS

The sound of the ship's bullhorn pulling into port was like sweet music to Alonzo's ears. The two hundred bricks on board the love boat was about to make Alonzo the most important man on the Chesapeake Bay, and pretty soon the entire Atlantic. Nothing motivated Alonzo more than money, and now that his ship had finally rolled in, he knew he would be in for more problems 'cause that's what more money usually brought.

Money had already caused him to kill his one time best friend, gotten his cousin kidnapped, his cousin's girlfriend killed and even caused chaos between him and his closest associate. Still, money was a necessary evil that Alonzo wasn't quite ready to give up yet. It truly ruled everything around him. He solemnly rubbed the stubble on his chin and reminisced of his broke days as his workers unloaded the crates of cocaine off the ship.

"Damn Eric man, we were supposed to do this together. This was our dream, baby, our dream!"

Alonzo suddenly felt a tear burn his right eye and roll down his cheek. It was the first time money and acquisition had made him regret his actions. Deep inside, Alonzo knew Eric was a good brother and didn't deserve to die, especially at the hands of him. How could he fault a man who shared the same ambition as him? Alonzo wondered if the Lord could ever forgive him for his sins, for he was the modern day Cain and Eric had been Able.

When the last of the kilos were unloaded and stored in the warehouse that he had disguised as a boating house, Alonzo sat alone on the edge of the pier. Somehow, Eric's family would reap the benefits of his success.

Back at Alonzo's house, Myra cut Mandy an evil look as Mandy rode Alonzo into a climatic coma. Tonight was one of Mandy's unusually freaky nights and she wasn't holding back any punches. Maybe it was all the millions of dollars Alonzo boasted about that turned her on. Whatever the case, one thing was for sure, she was putting in her money's worth tonight. She seduced, sucked, and fucked Alonzo better than she ever had before and now she was moving in for the grand finale. Mandy grinded her thick hips slowly on Alonzo, pulsating her vagina muscles just enough to make her victim go crazy.

"Oh shit, girl, here I come!" Alonzo shrieked in pleasure as he had quickly succumbed to Mandy's knockout pussy punch.

"Yeah, Daddy, come on!" Mandy screamed, attempting to share in Alonzo's ecstasy.

Myra sat back and watched the whole freak show in shear irritation. It wasn't that Mandy had outperformed her, they both had skills and always knew unique ways to please their men. It was the fact that Mandy was beginning to toy with her emotions. Ever since Myra confessed to Mandy about killing Karen for Alonzo, Mandy sensed Myra had a deep emotional attachment to Alonzo. Even though she never said it, Mandy intended on exploiting her sister's feelings every chance she got until Myra realized that Alonzo was just a very wealthy trick for them. That was rule number one for them, never fall in love with your clients. Clients never looked for love, they looked for sex, plenty of it, good and nasty. The nastier you were, the more they kept coming back, and Alonzo had been a true and faithful customer. Mandy couldn't believe Myra was so stupid to get involved in Alonzo's business matters, now the ball was in his court. That was rule number two Myra broke, never let a man control your heart, then he controls your mind.

Alonzo arose the next morning feeling more relaxed than he felt in years. He thought Mandy was the more refined of the twins, boy was he wrong. If Zo received any more pampering like this, he would have to be the first man in history to marry twin sisters, at the same time. Alonzo sensed Myra was acting a little strange last night. Maybe her and Mandy had a little beef earlier. Whatever it was, Alonzo didn't care. It was now his world and everybody else was just leasing it. He pulled out his cell phone and hesitated before he placed the call. Alonzo wasn't that good at apologizing.

"Hola," A Columbian accent sounded on the other line

"Hola amigo. Qué pasa?" Alonzo greeted Emilio as if he hadn't heard from him in years.

"Alonzo, my friend, I trust you received your shipment, no?"

"Yes, my friend, I have the package. I'm just calling once again to thank you for the opportunity to do business with you and to apologize for what went down during your classy party."

"Yes, your associate and his girlfriend are very rude, no? In my country, both of them would instantly be shot in the head for such insolence. They're lucky I'm a man of extreme patience."

"Yeah, I know, Emilio, but Reap's so wound up in that bitch he can't see the forest from the trees. He used to be straight business, no emotional attachments. Now he's acting like a weak ass punk over this bitch. I don't know, man, I might have to let him go."

"Well, I can't deal with him or his bitch. Never let them in my sight again Zo, or I will kill them. As for the coke, it's there anytime you want to do business with me. As long as you help me to get rich, I'll help you get rich."

"Gracias, my friend. Tu' es bueno hermano (You are a good man). I promise, you'll have no more problems from me. Only good business from now on, si?"

"Si, amigo, adios."

"Adios." Alonzo hung up the phone feeling refreshed that he didn't lose his new connect. Emilio had a point, Reap was getting weak and Thai was a little too feisty for comfort. A bitch like Thai could definitely ruin him and Reap. He would have to have a serious talk with Reap about his love life.

Mandy sarcastically smirked at her sister as Myra grabbed her overnight bag and headed for the front door. "Headed to your man's, oh, I mean our man's house tonight?"

Myra stopped in her tracks and slowly turned to face Mandy.

"Don't start with me tonight, bitch, I'm not for it."

"Watch who you calling a bitch, bitch! I just asked you a fuckin' question. Don't be so sensitive," Mandy said, switching her character from Diva to Drama Queen.

"Well, none of your damn business where I'm going, is that better?" Myra turned and stormed towards the door.

"Alright, killer," Mandy said, turning and brushing her long, jet black hair over her shoulder like she was competing for America's Top Model.

"Bitch!" Myra screamed, charging towards Mandy with rage. In an effort to get out of the way of her obviously deranged sister, Mandy turned to run; it was too late. With force, Myra grabbed a fistful of Mandy's silky locks and slung her to the floor. Straddling her wiggling body, Myra whaled away on Mandy's face, screaming uncontrollably. "You fake bitch, don't ever call me that again. I'll kill you!"

Myra blacked out. When she regained her senses, Mandy was knocked unconscious from her head being repeatedly banged against the hard wood floors of their lavish apartment. She realized that in an act of rage she had nearly killed her sister. All week long, Mandy had been tormenting Myra with smart comments of being in love with Alonzo and being his new hired assassin. She teased Myra about catching feelings in the bedroom and fucking up their hustle. Myra had enough of Mandy. She was sorry what she had done to Mandy, but at this point, she didn't care if they ever talked again. Myra got up from the floor, fixed her face in the bathroom mirror and grabbed her overnight bag once again. Even though she only had enough clothes for one night, she had the feeling she wouldn't be returning to their apartment any time soon.

Myra stepped out of the bathtub, her perfectly bronze body still glistening with remnants of soapsuds. Taking a sip of the pink champagne she had at her tub side, she seductively swayed in the room, her luscious body dripping wet. She slowly made eye contact with her target. "So tell me, what do you see in her."

"In who?" The mere sight of Myra butt-naked under candlelight made Alonzo dumbfounded.

"My sister. What do you see in her?"

"Same thing I see in you. Y'all twins, aren't you? What kind of question is that?" Alonzo snarled, irritated with Myra's line of questioning.

"No, what makes you like her more than me, after what I did for you?"

"Oh c'mon, Myra. Let's put that behind us, baby. That was a business transaction between us, that's all. You were compensated well. You can't take stuff like that personal, sweetheart. I don't like Mandy more than you either, baby. You know you're my favorite."

"I see the way you look at her, Zo, like you're infatuated with her. Eyes don't lie."

"Myra stop tripping. You're acting like you got feelings for me or something, what's the deal? Myra lowered her eyes to the ground like an innocent schoolgirl having her first crush on a boy.

"I've been thinking. You know what I did for you, the business transaction. Well…I, I'd like to make it full-time."

"What the fuck you talking about, Myra? Are you drunk?"

"Yes, but I'm speaking a sober mind. When I did that, it sent a rush that I can't describe through my body. I thought I would regret it, have nightmares about it and things. But I don't. I can't forget it. It's like I crave it. All my heartaches growing up; all my stored anger, my aggressions, got released when I inserted that needle in her. I felt redeemed." Myra playfully plopped her body against Alonzo's on the bed.

"Look, you don't know what you're asking. You're drunk and confused. Killing ain't you. What you did was just child's play compared to real contract killing. Let's forget this whole silly conversation and have some real fun." Alonzo kissed Myra's full lips and grabbed a handful of her voluptuous ass.

"Whatever," Myra hissed.

Slam! The sound of shattered glass broke the silence of the night. Alonzo instantly sprang up in the bed, scanning the room. Myra was still sound asleep. The shattered glass had come from downstairs. Alonzo crept out of the bed and reached for his .40 caliber that he always kept in his nightstand drawer. With caution, he made his way out the bedroom and down the stairs. Turning on the lights, Alonzo saw the glass that used to be his living room bay window shattered on the floor. He looked up to see a loaded 9mm to his head.

"You know what time it is, nigga. Turn off the light, drop the gun and go to the safe!" a voice blasted through a black ski mask. "Hurry up, I ain't got all day!"

"It's no safe in here, dawg. I'm not holding nothing. You got me confused." Alonzo tried to stay calm, but was jittery.

"Look, man, I'm gonna say this motherfuckin' shit one more motherfuckin' time. It's no secret you're banking. I know about the bricks you just copped from Columbia. A few thousand ain't gonna break you, nigga. Now, once again, I need to see that safe."

Alonzo walked downstairs to his office, all the while brainstorming for ideas to prevent opening the safe and giving the coward what he was looking for. Alonzo fumbled with the dial on the safe.

"Hurry up!" The voice seemed more impatient. "I'm not playing with you, nigga!"

"I forgot the combination. I'm trying to remember," Alonzo said, now sweating.

Alonzo suddenly saw a red dot appear on the safe and disappear. "Wait, man, I know the numbers…"

"Bam!" The man with the mask fell forward, his brains spilling from the mask that concealed his identity. Myra stood behind him with a smoking .40 cal Glock, the red dot still lit. Alonzo quickly lifted the mask off the intruder. It was

Malcolm, one of his workers down Fells Point who unloaded the bricks of coke off the ship for him the other day. Alonzo thought, *In this business you can't trust anyone, and I mean no one! Your grandma would rob you if given the right circumstances.* Alonzo didn't say a word. He just looked up at Myra and nodded his head.

CHAPTER FIFTEEN: THE END ALL

Reap tried hard as he could to forget about what happened in Miami. He couldn't. Truth was, he was more than ready to give his life for Thai if need be. The odds were stacked against him, and without a second thought, he was ready to die to defend her. Reap never thought that he could feel this way about another person again. He didn't care if she was a wanted murderer, as far as he was concerned, so was he.

Before Thai, the only person Reap would consider dying for was Regina, and even that was questionable. He often wondered if the outcome would've been the same if he never left Regina for the military. Would Regina still be alive? Would he have killed Glenn? Would Glenn have killed them both? Reap tried not to dwell in the past. After all, you had to learn to live with regrets. All Reap knew was that Thai had to be super special for him to risk life and limb. He couldn't let a love like that get away, not again.

Reap had a special night planned for him and Thai. He made reservations at her favorite restaurant, Pieces, located on the 6th floor of the Hyatt. He ordered a dozen long stem roses from the best florist he could find. He even washed and waxed Alonzo's candy-apple red Mercedes 600SL for him to borrow tonight, something he never did. It was never in Reap's style to flex someone else's shit. However, tonight was different. Tonight was the night he would ask Thai to be his bride.

Reap's nerves were on pins and needles. It's funny, he could murder a motherfucka he never seen before and have a good night's rest, but when it came to Thai, he was like a kid on the first day of kindergarten. He wanted everything to be perfect. Reap's final touch would be the ten carat diamond ring he bought that put a major dent in his savings. Now she would have to accept his proposal, at least, think long and hard about it.

Reap picked Thai up at 6:00 sharp. He was decked in his black Armani suit, complete with matching dress hat. Reap only wore a suit for extra special occasions; he preferred baggy jeans and T-shirts. In his line of work, he had to be comfortable. Thai stepped out the house wearing her black Donna Karen dress with the high split in front. The two matched perfectly. Reap affectionately kissed Thai on her cheek so that he wouldn't smear her plum Mac lipstick she had just applied.

"You look lovely tonight, sweetheart," Reap said with a proud smile on his face.

"You're not looking so bad yourself, loverman," Thai said, grabbing Reap's head and planting a wet, juicy, slobbering kiss on his lips. "Fuck this lipstick, you're my baby."

"Ready for a special night, sweetie?" Reap said, now blushing a little.

"Been waiting all day, Daddy, let's go."

As Reap and Thai awaited their meal in the trendy restaurant, Thai wondered why Reap was all of the sudden so romantic. Though they were always intimate, Reap was never big on romance and sensitivity; he thought it was a sign of weakness. At this point, Thai was so turned on by Reap that her panties were beginning to moisten. She wanted him now. Thai excused herself to the lady's room to get herself together. Reaped used this time to make his way to the D.J. booth to request a song. When Thai returned to the table, she was hornier than ever. "Let's get out of here, baby, I want you now."

"Hold on, baby, we haven't eaten yet."

"I don't care, I need you now."

"In a second, pooh. I have something planned for us first." Reap raised his hand and motioned to the D.J. R. Kelly's, "Forever", began to play.

"Hey, Ms. Beloved, we are gathered here, to join each other hand in hand..."

As R. Kelly belted out the tune, Reap pulled a black box from his pocket. As soon as R. Kelly sang the words, "Marry me, marry me, marry me, marry me." Reap took the diamond platinum ring from the case and placed it on Thai's left ring finger. She was speechless. Tears began to stream down her face, making her perfectly applied mascara run down as well.

"Well, will you?" Reap said, wiping Thai's face with the cloth napkins placed at the table.

"Will I...Will I what?" Thai said, composing herself.

"What the Pied Piper said, marry me."

"I...I don't...Yes, baby, I will. I will marry you. I love you so much." Thai rose from her seat and took Reap by the hand, standing him to his feet. She passionately hugged his neck and gave him an intense, knee-weakening kiss that screamed, *I gonna fuck the shit outta you when we get home.*

All the patrons in the restaurant stood in unison and

applauded. Some even whistled and screamed, "You go, girl, get your man." It was romantic. The manager gave the two dinner on the house as an engagement present. The evening was perfect. Reap couldn't believe he was now engaged to the most beautiful woman in the world. His life was now complete. As for the murder game, he was done. He and Thai had a long talk and both decided to go straight and legit from here on out. They would put their money together and go into a husband and wife bounty hunting business together. Thai would still keep her Real Estate business and with Reap's help it would expand. Together, it was nothing they couldn't do. As long as their past didn't catch up with them.

Reap and Thai packed their bags for a spur-of-the-moment trip to Punta Canta. With all they been through in the last couple days, they deserved a vacation. Reap called Alonzo to take them to the airport. Alonzo was very bitter that Reap was leaving the game for a mysterious bitch he barely knew. Over the years, Reap had evolved from a contractor, to an associate, to a friend of Alonzo's and he found it hard to deal with losing a real friend. *This was some real bitch shit Reap was on,* Alonzo thought. Throwing away an opportunity to become a billionaire's top assassin for some scandalous broad, he couldn't see it. But it was Reap's life and Alonzo would be less of a friend if he didn't support him, so he did.

"I'm on my way, man," Alonzo told Reap hesitantly.

"Oh, tell him to bring the Escalade, baby. I have a lot of bags," Thai said, grinning from ear to ear.

"Bring the Escalade, Zo, we need the room for the bags," Reap repeated.

"Done. Be there in a half." Alonzo hung up the phone.

Alonzo drove slowly to the airport. In his mind flashed all of the important hits Reap made for him over the years. Hits that would have meant Alonzo's freedom if they hadn't been carried out. He thought about deadly business transactions that, if it wasn't for Reap having his back, would've went bad for him and possibly meant his death. He thought about Reap helping him get his cousin back from New York in one piece, minus the missing ring finger. Alonzo couldn't let him go, not like this. Not without having a serious sit-down with him first. How could he have let this bitch weaken him so much? As Alonzo pulled into the airport parking lot, he looked over at Reap.

"We gotta talk."

"Go head, homey, talk," Reap said, gathering his bags to exit the car.

"Alone," Alonzo emphasized.

"Go 'head, boys. Y'all talk and say your goodbyes. It was nice knowing you, Alonzo, and I'll never forget you for being Reap's friend. Any friend of his is a friend of mines. Take care." Thai gave Alonzo a tight hug and kiss on his cheek. "I'll be waiting in the terminal, sweetie," Thai said as she exited the truck.

All night long Thai had been wrestling with her decision. Up to this point, she had played the role so well that the Oscars would have passed up Julia Roberts, Halle Berry, and Meryl Streep to give her an award. She was simply astonishing. Truth was, she was an international assassin, employed by Emilio Sanchez. That was who ordered the hit on Devon "D-Coy" McCoy because he was too ambitious and was threatening Emilio's status of being the number one supplier on the Eastern coast. The day before her return back home to New York, her husband Eric Little was brutally and cowardly killed after planning a surprise "Welcome Home" party for her at the Marriott Hotel. She found out from grimy Swayze that those cowards were some Baltimore cats named Marco "Reap" Raymond and Alonzo Stewart. Thai swore that she would go to her grave to avenge Eric, her first real love. She went as far as setting up the meeting between Alonzo and Emilio in Miami to stake her revenge. Though she did care for Reap, it was nothing like the love she had for her Elite. She could never allow herself to get married to another man, especially the motherfucka that murdered her husband and the father of her only two year old son. She never even had a chance to tell Eric she was a hired assassin. She kept it from him cleverly for four years with the Real Estate agent front. He simply never questioned her integrity, that was the kind of man Eric was. With a tear in her green eyes, Thai whispered, "This is for you Eric baby, so long boyz."

Thai pressed the remote between her fingers. Within seconds she heard a fiery "Kaboom!" She held her ears tightly and turned to look. All she saw was fire and scattered debris of a once fine Escalade. Smiling to herself, Thai thought as she turned and walked away towards the terminal, "You always Reap what you sow," and "He who lives by the sword, shall die by the sword."

Thai gracefully walked to the terminal in preparation for her flight to Punta Canta. As she handed her ticket to the attendant, she was approached by two plain clothes Federal Agents. "Ms. Thailand Little, we need to talk to you about a murder that happened in Kingston, Jamaica. Come with us."

Thai couldn't believe her luck. Through all her struggle to right the wrong that was done to her, her story wasn't going to have a happy ending after all. What about her 2 year old son that desperately needed her in New York? He already didn't have a father, now he might not have a mother as well. What about her sweet and much deserved revenge? Was it now all in vain? Following the agents through the airport, Thai now whispered to herself, "I guess, she who lives by the sword, dies by the sword."

9 781424 163595